There I Find Rest

Strawberry Sands Book One

Jessie Gussman

Published By: Jessie Gussman

Contents

Acknowledgements   VI

1. Chapter 1   1

2. Chapter 2   24

3. Chapter 3   45

4. Chapter 4   53

5. Chapter 5   72

6. Chapter 6   91

7. Chapter 7   117

8. Chapter 8   128

9. Chapter 9   147

10. Chapter 10   159

11. Chapter 11   175

12. Chapter 12   185

13. Chapter 13   209

14. Chapter 14   233

15. Chapter 15   255

16. Chapter 16   276

17. Chapter 17   292

18. Chapter 18   319

19. Chapter 19   347

20. Chapter 20   373

21. Chapter 21   386

22. Chapter 22   410

23. Chapter 23   435

24. Chapter 24   452

25. Chapter 25   477

26. Chapter 26   492

27. Chapter 27   504

28. Chapter 28   520

Epilogue   536

There I Find Peace   546

A Gift from Jessie   571

Acknowledgements

Cover art by Kim Killion of The Killion Group
Editing by Heather Hayden
Narration by Jay Dyess
Author Services by CE Author Assistant

Listen to a FREE professionally per-formed and produced audiobook ver-sion of this title on Youtube. Search for "Say With Jay" to browse all available FREE Dyess/Gussman audiobooks.

Chapter 1

Kim stood on the walk and looked at the cottage she had inherited from her mother.

Blue, with creamy white shutters, the paint was slightly faded, but it was in much better condition than what she had expected. The stable off to the side looked far better than she had expected as well, although the big barn farther back looked weather-beaten and was missing a few boards.

Because of her cancer, her mother had not been able to be at the cottage for the last few months of her life, so Kim hadn't been sure what to expect.

Her mother had purchased the cottage and stable along the shores of Lake Michigan after Kim had left the house.

She'd never spent any time here, and her mother hardly ever talked about them.

From what Kim understood, her mother had occasionally rented the cottage out, with the tenant getting a discount on the rent to do upkeep on the stable.

That's all Kim knew, and now, considering that she just buried her mother...well, the woman she thought was her mother all of her life...she could hardly get more information now.

She took a breath and adjusted her purse strap where it lay slung over her shoulder. Her mother had died.

Not really. Not truly. The woman who gave birth to her was still alive.

She still hadn't quite gotten used to the idea that she had parents. A mother and father who hadn't known about her until less than a month ago.

They loved her, they had all her life, and she felt the same about them. But to love someone was one thing, to have them be your parents was a completely different ball game. Kim wasn't sure how to move forward from there. There was no roadmap for them.

She put a hand over her rounded belly and looked at the small cottage again.

She was going to be a mother, the second time over. This time, instead of having a distant husband who didn't care about her at all and who cheated on her as well as belittled and neglected her, she would be alone.

Which was worse?

She wasn't entirely sure. She supposed it said something about her character, or maybe her courage, since she figured that being alone should be better, but she wasn't sure it was.

At least when she had a husband, she had the illusion of having someone to lean on.

Now it was just her.

And God.

Maybe she'd draw closer to the Almighty here on this secluded beach.

It wasn't far outside of Strawberry Sands, just two hundred yards up the beach from where the main street ended at the dunes. Strawberries Sands was tiny, though, and the beach house felt like it was miles away from civilization.

She wouldn't care if it were.

Except for… She touched her stomach again, placing a hand protectively over it. She couldn't leave society and raise her child in isolation. Even though that's what she felt like she wanted for herself.

If there was one thing she learned in her over forty years of life, it was she couldn't live her life for herself.

She'd taken one night, one crazy, regretful, sad, exhilarating night, for herself, and now she had a new life to be responsible for.

The idea of giving that new life up for adoption crossed her mind more than once. She was forty for goodness' sake. Divorced. With a child who was supposed to be going to college but who had decided to go to LA and become an actress instead.

Almost as though thinking about Alyssa had conjured her up, her phone rang with the specific ringtone that indicated it was her wayward daughter.

Still standing on the porch, she dug it out of her purse, for some reason not wanting to step into the cottage. Maybe delaying the inevitable. It would smell like her mother. Surely. It would have her mother's touches in it.

Not her mother.

She couldn't get that thought to settle into her brain. Iva May had been her mother in every way. But the secret she finally disclosed shortly before she died had turned Kim's world upside down.

"Hello?" She held the phone to her ear and turned toward the lake, the deep blue of the sky meeting a more gray-blue of the chilly Lake Michigan in late March. Even though it was a warm day, the lake would still be in the forties, cold and unwelcoming, except it was beautiful and compelling and inspiring, too.

Kim took a long breath through her nose as her daughter began to speak.

"Mom! You didn't answer my text."

No. She hadn't.

"Can you send it right now? I need it right away."

She wanted to tell her daughter to come home. Come home and she would finance whatever transportation cost it took to get her from LA to the Eastern shore of Lake Michigan. But she knew better. Her daughter and she had already had that conversation, and she'd lost. But sending money seemed to be enabling her.

"I didn't answer your text because we've already talked about this," she said softly, trying to fight back the hurt in her heart. She wanted to send her daughter as much money as she needed. Money for whatever she needed. But if her daughter wasn't able to make ends meet in LA, if she was spending above her means or unable to earn what she needed to survive, then maybe that was the Lord saying LA wasn't for her.

She'd already sent $4000 over the last month.

It wasn't that she couldn't afford it, although she really couldn't. Her divorce settlement had not been generous, and her husband had fought over every penny.

Of course, he had the new family he'd already started, the woman who was pregnant when their divorce became final was now his wife, and he wanted to keep as much as he could to finance his new start.

"We talked about it, and you were being unreasonable. I thought maybe you would have seen my side by now." Her daughter was most definitely irritated with her.

"Did you ask your dad?"

At Iva May's funeral, Alyssa had walked in holding onto her dad's arm, with the new wife, who was just three years older than Alyssa and eight months pregnant, holding onto his other arm. He looked like the quintessential family man. Which of course had made Kim feel like the biggest loser in the world, since not only had he not been a family man, he hadn't been any kind of husband and father to speak of while he was married to her. She couldn't ever remember attending a funeral hanging on his arm. If anything, she arrived with Alyssa long before he showed up, sat in the back, and left as soon as everything was over. Most of the time, he didn't even see her or talk to her.

That was the story of their marriage.

"Dad said he paid you enough in the settlement that you should be able to take care of me for the rest of my life and I could live in the lap of luxury. I know he's loaded. And he gave it all to you. In fact, he told me that he gave so much to you that he can barely support his new wife and their baby. Mom, how could you take so much from him? Don't you know they have a child to support? What are you, jealous of his new wife because she's young and beautiful when you're old and wrinkled and fat?"

Kim swallowed.

"I'm sorry. I need to go. I... I just arrived at my destination." She swallowed again. "I love you."

She didn't give Alyssa a chance to answer before she swiped her phone off.

Turning around, she sat down on the top step, put her hands around her knees, and put her head in her arms, the tears silently dripping down her face.

She never even told Alyssa about her new sister.

She was just into her third trimester. Three months to go in the pregnancy. She was showing more now, but a month ago when she saw Alyssa at her mother's funeral—Iva May's funeral—she hadn't been showing enough for anyone to be sure, and the loose blouse she had worn had hid any hints of a protruding stomach.

The entire town of Blueberry Beach had been in mourning over the loss of one of their matriarchs, and no one had paid any attention to Kim's figure. If she had gained a little weight while her mother was dying of cancer, no one would blame her.

That wasn't really the problem. Of course.

It wasn't even the insults that Alyssa had just uttered. She was a child. Nineteen years old and thought she knew everything, but she knew nothing.

Kim had been the same at one point and had had the same mentality. Thought she knew everything.

It wasn't really that, either.

It wasn't that the insults had been designed to hurt and wound, to be so nasty and mean that they would strike pain into the recipient, repeated from what Alyssa had heard her father saying about Kim.

Of course they were mean, but the main reason that they were so successful in hurting Kim was because they were accurate.

She was jealous. Jealous of her ex's new wife. The wife that her daughter and ex seemed to adore, to slather attention on, and to hold in high esteem.

She didn't hold a torch for Todd, not at all. But it made her feel like there was something terribly wrong with her that he was capable of affection, of attention, of love and could lavish it so freely on someone. He just was incapable of giving it to Kim.

He somehow managed to turn everything around and make it all her fault. He'd even managed to make the fact that she'd been caught with his business partner, Davis, sound like she'd been cheating on him. When her one-night stand, the one night where she'd lived for herself instead of thinking about everybody else, had been well after the finalization of their divorce.

Todd was the one who had been cheating on her all along. He was the one whose girlfriend was pregnant when he served her with divorce papers. He was the one who had neglected his family, his wife.

But she was the one who paid the price. She had always been the one to pay the price. It didn't seem fair.

But Alyssa had hit the nail on the head. Kim was jealous. Bitter. Frustrated. Sad.

And confused. If a forty-year-old could still be confused.

Her mother wasn't who she thought she was, and she didn't know where she belonged in the world anymore. No husband, no mom, no home.

She tried to shove down the fear that clenched around her backbone, squeezing hard. Harder and more forceful when she thought about how she was alone, unloved, and uncared for.

Even though Bev and Bill - apparently her real parents - would love to have a relationship with her, it wasn't the same. Just...she didn't feel a natural, unfeigned connection deep in her soul the way a lifetime relationship with a person's parents should feel.

No fault of theirs.

She stood, embarrassed that she'd succumbed to the need to cry, and so close to her destination. She could have at least gone inside the cottage for privacy.

Not that there was anyone walking on the beach, despite the unusual warmth of the March afternoon.

Lifting her head, she looked straight at the stable. It was in decent condition, and when she'd decided to leave everything and come here, she had the idea that she could rent horses to paying tourists. Give them a few happy hours riding on the beach. Make beautiful memories with their families, sweet times for everyone.

Still, the thought didn't stir her like it had. Not with the feeling of being alone.

You are never alone.

She closed her eyes. God was with her. She knew that. She'd known that since she was little, but for a while, she'd walked away from that idea. Bought into the ideas of the world. After all, Todd had laughed at anything that had to do with any type of Christian thoughts or actions. He scoffed at her religion, made fun of her "crutch," which was what he called her need for God and her dependence on Jesus.

Lord, I feel like I'm using You now. Coming back to You when I'm scared and alone. After I left You when I had everything. A husband, even if he didn't really care for me, a beautiful child, a great house, and lots of money.

Her eyes filled with tears again, and she took a minute to blink them away. Some people thought she'd had the perfect life. She would have said that too. After all, a person didn't expect everything in their life to be completely like their dreams. Just because she didn't have the intimate, beautiful relationship she always dreamed about with her husband didn't mean that the rest of her life wasn't amazing. She laughed. Most of it anyway.

Now, it was all gone, and it felt like she was just using God as a genie of sorts if she turned to Him when she had nothing left. She wouldn't appreciate it if someone did that to her.

I want to get my life back together, but I feel like I need to earn the right to come back before I turn to You. After all, I didn't have a lot of time for You when there wasn't really anything I needed.

She'd been resisting turning to the Lord for a while for that very reason.

Shoving those thoughts aside, wiping the rest of the moisture off her face, she pushed to her feet. She was getting clumsy, awkward, with her belly leading the way. She hated the last months of pregnancy. Some pregnant ladies glowed with impending motherhood.

She was the opposite. Instead, she looked exhausted and sallow, fat and ungainly.

Shoving her phone back in her purse, she grabbed the key to the cottage and turned to go up the rest of the steps.

This was a new start. A new life. She wasn't going to let fear, or insecurity, or what anyone said about her hold her back.

She was going to start all over again, even if she was forty.

She had the key in her hand, lifting it to put it in the lock when, to her great surprise, the door opened.

A man stood in the doorway, his hair casually ruffled, a tight T-shirt stretching over broad shoulders and jeans slung low on his hips.

Several days' worth of stubble bristled on his cheeks, but it was those eyes, deep and dark and so very blue, that gave her pause for just a moment, and then she recognized him.

Davis. The father of her child.

Chapter 2

Davis stared at the woman on the step in front of him.

He had been expecting her. He'd found out, shamelessly using various contacts that he'd gotten through his years in business, that her mother owned this cottage. He also found out that Kim's Aunt Tricia had basically stolen her mother's house in Blueberry Beach out from underneath her, and Kim had let it go.

That made sense to him. That was the kind of person Kim was. She wasn't a fighter, she didn't strive, she was kind to a fault and generous even beyond that.

Davis had had to bite his tongue more than once as Todd, his soon-to-be ex-business partner, had neglected her, treated her terribly, and only paraded her around when he thought it would benefit him.

Davis had seen Todd cheat on Kim more than once, and it had made his throat just burn and his fingers clench every time.

The man didn't know what a gem he had.

He certainly didn't know how to treat people, least of all his wife.

Of course, that didn't excuse what Davis had done six months ago.

He held Todd in derision, but he had ended up being no better.

"It's good to see you again, Kim." Davis kept his voice pitched low and couldn't believe how normal it sounded. Considering that he was sure if he took his one hand out of his pocket or pulled his other off the doorknob, they'd be shaking like leaves in a storm.

"Davis. I wasn't expecting you here," Kim said, her hand at her throat, before she lifted her chin, as though determined to march forward, and grabbed her purse strap, like she needed something to hold onto.

He certainly did. He had a death grip on the doorknob, but she couldn't see his white knuckles from her side, and he certainly wasn't going to tell her that seeing her had affected him far more than he thought it would.

Especially since she really wouldn't have been expecting him. Maybe she hoped to never see him again. It was an idea he couldn't stand. Which was why, the evening of their one-night stand, which he hadn't meant to have at all, he approached her, knowing that she had been divorced from Todd and hoping that enough time had elapsed that she might welcome someone new in her life, since he'd admired her from afar ever since he'd met her.

Regardless, the events of that night had caused him to back way off. It was the first and only time either one of them had done such a thing.

He regretted it, not just because it was wrong, but because it wasn't the way he'd wanted to treat her when he'd approached her. He'd wanted to take things slow and give her the attention and affection and respect and friendship she deserved. She was worth a lifetime, not just a night.

After his big mess-up, he wasn't sure how to start over. Could one ever really start over when he'd already done something so terrible?

Renting the house from her mother was the only thing he could think of that might possibly help them to meet again without him seeming like a stalker, although this was definitely skirting the edges of that.

After her divorce, she certainly didn't run in circles that included Todd, other than her mother's funeral. Davis had attended, even though he had never met her mother and probably shouldn't have gone. It wasn't like he could stay away.

"I take it you don't know I signed a year lease for this cottage from your mother?"

Her eyes grew big, and she didn't have to shake her head for him to know that this was a total surprise to her.

"I have the lease agreement in my brief-case over by the desk. I can show you if you don't believe me."

"I... I believe you." She sounded a little breathless, like he'd punched her in the stomach instead of telling her that he was renting her house. He wasn't quite sure why this would be so upsetting for her unless... He'd heard her Aunt Tricia had swindled her out of her mother's house. Surely with the great settlement that Todd had told everyone he'd given her she had plenty of money to afford something else.

Unless, of course, Todd lied.

"You look a little...odd. Would you like to sit down?" He opened the door wider, hardly daring to think she would come in. But he must have given her a more stunning blow than what he realized, because she wandered in, almost as though he hadn't invited her, but like she was seeing the place for the first time, looking around, walking slowly, the way one would walk in a museum, not into a house they were familiar with.

"Haven't you ever been here before?"

She took a breath and said, "No."

Her throat worked, like she was pushing past something, and then she looked at him. "I just recently learned about it. I... I was planning on living here. When is your lease up?"

"I have six more months."

It hurt his heart the way she looked disappointed. Like that had been a shock and an unwelcome surprise.

He knew, having lived almost forty years, that sometimes a person liked someone, really liked them, maybe even loved them, and the feelings were not returned. It had happened more than once to him, people he would have enjoyed being friends with just weren't interested in being friends with him. A few different times, he had been casually interested in ladies and his interest had not been returned.

"Is that a problem?" he asked, not wanting to but also knowing that the look on her face indicated that there was some kind of issue.

In fact, as he looked closer, her lashes seemed to be wet, and he almost wondered if... Maybe she had been sitting on the steps crying.

He'd heard her pull in and waited for her to knock. Not wanting to open the door and possibly scare her away before she had made it to the door.

He had wondered if she'd known he lived there and if she was trying to get her nerve up to see him.

He supposed he had been engaging in denial or some kind of fantasy, because he almost had himself convinced that she had come, knowing he lived there, and had wanted to see him again.

Such was not the case. Obviously.

"I… I was planning on living here. I… I suppose you find it hard to believe, but I don't have anywhere else to go."

That set off some warning bells in his head. Todd had bragged about what a huge settlement he'd given his first wife. Complained was more like it, although Todd loved to brag about what a family man he was, which was odd, since no one who knew him would say he was a great husband or dad.

Davis had a good idea that Kim could back that up with facts.

"What about the home Todd gave you in the divorce settlement?" His eyes narrowed as her widened eyes confirmed his suspicions.

She knew nothing about it.

"There was no home," she stated flatly.

He pursed his lips. He should have known, after all the lying Todd had done, that wouldn't be true either.

She huffed out a breath. "I suppose he told you there was?" Her lips flattened, like it was his fault for believing Todd. And he supposed he couldn't blame her for being annoyed. After all, if anyone knew what a liar Todd was, he did.

"Right." He nodded. His fingers tightened on the doorknob. "I suppose there was no money either?"

"Enough to pay off my share of the debts he incurred. That was it."

"I see."

She probably knew about the lies Todd had been telling. He knew Alyssa, their daughter, thought her mom was rich. And she thought so because her dad said so. Saying that Kim had taken more money than he could afford to pay, and he had to struggle to provide a decent home for his new wife and child. Davis had heard him tell Alyssa that he couldn't afford to give her any money, so she needed to hit up her mother, because her mother had soaked him in the divorce.

He hardly thought Kim would be here, at this small cottage, hoping to live here, if she had as much money as Todd said.

He finally had the presence of mind to close the door behind her and lead her to one of the stools in the kitchen.

She followed him, seeming to be deep in thought, and sat down when he indicated.

"Would you be willing to end your lease early?" she asked, giving him a direct gaze with no guile in it. There was no flirt, and there was no hint of the night they'd spent together.

He supposed it shouldn't surprise him. After all, she'd lost her mother, and if the rumors that he had heard were correct, she'd found out that the woman who died wasn't even her birth mother. Not only that, but her daughter had quit college and was in LA, constantly broke, if Todd were to be believed. She'd been divorced, gotten very little out of it, and was swindled out of the home that her mother had lived in by a family member.

Now, what looked to be like her last hope seemed to be fading in front of her eyes. He could see that almost as clearly as though it were happening to him.

There was something about Kim that made him feel compassion coupled with a deep desire to help.

But as much as he wanted to help her, he wasn't going to end his lease. That was the only thing tying him to her.

"No."

Her face fell at his answer, although she tried to hide her disappointment by pressing her lips together and nodding.

The answer was so simple, he almost didn't need to think about it before his mouth opened and the words came out.

"But I'm only using one bedroom. The smallest. If you'd like to use one of the other two, you're welcome to."

Her mouth dropped, and she looked offended.

"You want me to move in with you?" Her eyes narrowed, and she began shaking her head immediately. "No. Absolutely not. That's... That's..." Still shaking her head, she stood from the stool. "Obviously, you got the exact wrong idea of me. I understand how you could have gotten confused." She seemed to stumble, then caught herself. "Considering what happened the last time we were together." She bit her lip. "That... That was a mistake. Sorry."

"I'm the one who should be apologizing," he said immediately with no hesitation. It was true. Maybe he should lead with that. "I wasn't asking you to live with me. I wasn't asking anything of the sort, just trying to figure out how we can get this squared away, without me losing my home and still enabling you to have one."

"I think there was an apartment above the stable. That would be enough for me." Her voice sounded thoughtful, like she was talking to herself and not necessarily to him. Like she had pushed the night they shared together under the rug, not wanting to think about it at all. And he could understand that. He was embarrassed about it too. He probably wouldn't have said anything if it hadn't been for her mentioning it. It wasn't what he usually did, wasn't the way he usually treated anyone, especially someone he thought so much of. But that night had been...magical.

"There is an apartment above the stable, but if anybody's moving out to that, it will be me." That was a no-brainer. At least he'd be close to her, if nothing else. And he couldn't allow her to move while he stayed in the house. Moving would be the right thing to do, although it wasn't the way he was raised; it was the way he wanted to treat her.

Of course there was one other solution.

Before he could think it through, the words came to his lips. "We could get married." That would solve the problem of there being an issue with them living together. But from the look on her face, it wasn't a solution she wanted to entertain, not even for a second.

"No." She didn't elaborate, and he felt a sharper sense of disappointment than he expected. "I'll check the stable."

"No. I'll move there."

"No. It was never my intention to make anyone move."

"This is your home. It is the only one you have; you have every right to expect to live here. I'll need a bit of time to move my things."

He didn't allow her to argue with him anymore but turned toward the hall that led to the stairway where the three small bedrooms were located.

"But—" Her voice came from behind him, but he didn't stop walking. There was no way he was going to allow her to move into the stable while he stayed in the house. That had never been his intention. He hadn't given much thought to his suggestions, especially living to-gether, other than he didn't want her to go, he wanted to see her again. Now that he had, he wanted to see her more, but even if he hadn't felt like that, he couldn't force a person to move out of their home, not when he had the penthouse in Chicago with a gorgeous view of Lake Michigan and a large estate south of Chicago.

He wasn't quite sure how things were going to work out, but seeing Kim again had intensified all the feelings that he felt the last time he saw her at her mother's funeral. He definitely needed to see what he could do to see if she could feel the same.

Chapter 3

Kim stood in the entryway in the kitchen, watching the departing back of the man who answered the door. The father of her baby. The whole time he stood there, she felt a deep and abiding guilt that he didn't know.

She could say she didn't have his contact info, so she couldn't tell him, and that was accurate. Although, she certainly could go through Todd to get it.

Then Todd would want to know why, and so far, no one knew.

No one except Iva May, who passed away, and her, apparently, real parents.

They wanted to help her, would love to help her, but she just needed some time to think. It felt like her life had completely fallen apart.

And now, to make her feel even worse, like she needed that, she was apparently evicting this man out of his house.

The man she had a one-night stand with. The father of her baby. The man who was her ex-husband's business partner.

That last part made her want to run from the house, to go somewhere, anywhere other than here.

Maybe she would feel better if she knew what he really thought of her. Did he believe her when she'd told him she'd never done anything like that before? Did he think that was the way she was? That she was just like Todd?

He offered to marry you.

He had no idea what that had done to her. There was a part of her that desperately wanted to take him up on it. He didn't even know about the baby.

But of course, that wasn't the reason he offered. It was just out of convenience so that neither one of them would have to live above the stable.

She looked around the small cottage. She didn't want to share it with someone she wasn't married to. Everything in her rebelled against that. Just like everything in her rebelled against the idea of having a one-night stand.

The one time in her life she'd done it, she'd gotten caught, red-handed it seemed.

Never again. She wasn't going to compromise her convictions no matter how bad she felt or how much she wanted to walk away from life.

Definitely a person reaped what they sowed.

Well, she was going to reap, because she didn't have a choice, but she was going to be a lot more careful about what she sowed from here on out.

So, was she really going to allow Davis to move out to the stable, or was she going to entertain his idea of marriage?

Before she made any decisions about that, she probably ought to sit down and tell him about the baby. That was the right thing to do.

It was one thing for her to say she didn't have his contact info and couldn't tell him, it was a completely different thing for her to live beside him for any length of time and not tell him. The idea made her stomach cramp and her heart twirl, skipping beats and running ahead and making her feel lightheaded.

She took two steps back to the kitchen counter and sat down on the stool.

She needed to tell him. Right now. Waiting would only make it worse. He was going to be upset enough as it was. The problem was, she wanted to tell him and then never see him again. She didn't want to tell him, then have him living above the stable where she would run into him on a weekly, if not daily, basis almost certainly.

She wasn't sure how long she sat there, but eventually his footsteps sounded on the stairs and then in the hall as he came closer. Pushing herself up from the cozy kitchen stool, she took a second to admire the kitchen with the big windows that faced the lake and sheer curtains that would blow gently in the lake breeze this summer. She braced herself, glancing around for something to focus on.

The cottage was decorated beautifully, lakeside colors of blues and greens with soft cream throws on the recliner and the loveseat.

"Davis?" she said as he walked into the room, realizing she was wringing her hands together and forcing herself to stop.

"Kim?"

She had to fight not to close her eyes at the sound of her name on his lips. It sent a shiver down her back, clear to her toes, where it turned and caused her entire body to warm.

She straightened her hands, flexing her fingers, forcing her arms to hang at her sides, even though she wanted to cross them against her chest, protection against what was surely going to be an unpleasant experience.

He stood looking at her, his brows raised, his deep blue eyes holding hers with questions all through them. Those amazing, caring, kind, soul-reaching blue, blue eyes.

Chapter 4

Kim didn't have any great plans for what she was going to say. Hadn't really thought about the situation she was in now—facing the man who didn't know he was the father of her unborn child. Sure, she'd thought about telling him, knew she needed to, sometime in the future when she finally contacted him, but...she never thought about what she would do in any detail.

But now he was standing in front of her, looking at her with those eyes that she knew all too well she could easily get lost in, seeming to have endless patience while she shifted and stalled.

She opened her mouth, figuring she would just say, you're the father of the baby I'm going to have in three months, but before she could get any words out, there was a knock at the door.

She hadn't even heard a car pull in.

She glanced toward the door, grateful for the reprieve. In the window, she could see the two people who claimed to be her parents.

Bev and Bill. They actually were her parents, but that didn't negate the fact that Iva May had raised her.

It wasn't that she wasn't happy to see them. They were good people, and before she had known that they were her parents, she had liked them. She still did. But adjusting to the fact that her entire life had changed, shifted, irrevocably so, just took some getting used to.

"I don't recognize them. Do you?" Davis said from beside her, closer than he had been. She hadn't noticed that he'd taken a step forward, and he leaned toward her, almost as though protecting her.

The idea made her smile briefly. Never in her life had she had anyone who had wanted to protect her. To keep her safe. Cherish her. She thought those were little-girl dreams, and now that she was an older woman, although not too old to have a baby, she had given up on the idea of that ever happening. It only happened in movies and romance novels.

"Yes. They're my...parents." She stumbled over the word. He surely noticed, but he didn't say anything.

He paused as though trying to decide if he should stay or go. Finally he said, "All right, I'll let you handle them. I'm going to go out and get settled in the loft."

"You don't—"

He walked away from her, and she closed her mouth. What was she going to do? Offer to let him live with her? Offer to live somewhere else? Say that she was going out to the stable? She didn't have anywhere else to go.

And she didn't want to bring her baby home to a loft. She didn't know the heating situation, but in Michigan, there definitely needed to be some kind of good insulation and dependable heat if she was going to raise a child.

Davis opened the door and coolly introduced himself to Bev and Bill, who looked a little surprised.

Both of them held bags of what looked like groceries in their hands, and they both shifted so they could shake when Davis held out his hand.

He was humble and respectful, while not groveling.

"I didn't realize there was someone living here," Bill said, and his words didn't sound accusatory, but he definitely sounded like a concerned father.

Kim smiled to herself, just because she was forty years old and she'd never had a concerned father in her life before.

In Bill's defense, he thought she died at birth.

"I rented from Iva May before she passed away. I didn't realize that Kim was going to come out here and live. So, in order to give her space, I offered to move above the stable. I'm sure it's just a temporary thing until one of us finds a different place."

"You have a signed lease?" Bill asked, his intelligent eyes assessing the man in front of him from behind the wire rims of his glasses.

"I do. It's in my briefcase, and I can get it out and show you if you want me to." Davis did not sound defensive. They could be having a conversation about the weather or boating on the lake.

"You don't have to. I'm sure there's a copy in Iva May's things as well, we just haven't gotten to that point yet. Or per-haps we missed it because none of us realized there was a tenant here." There was a slight lift to Bill's brows as he looked her way, as though asking if she knew.

She shook her head. Of course she didn't know. She wouldn't have planned to move in if she had.

They'd moved all of Iva May's things out of her home because Aunt Tricia had demanded that she take it over, and Kim hadn't had time, or the fortitude, to go through everything.

Kim hadn't thought about fighting about the house, hadn't wanted to create waves in the family, and wasn't sure she wanted to live in Blueberry Beach anyway. She...wanted a brand-new start. But it seemed like she couldn't get away from her past. So much of it was standing in this room with her right now.

Davis, a bag slung over his back and a bag in one hand as well as his briefcase, said a few more words before stepping out the door and walking toward the stable.

Bev and Bill exchanged a look before they walked in and closed the door behind them.

"I didn't know," Kim felt like she had to say.

"Of course you didn't. None of us did. I... He looks familiar, that's all." Bev still seemed thoughtful.

Kim figured there was no point in trying to hide. She had already told her...parents about the baby. Iva May knew as well before she passed away. What they didn't know was who the father was.

"Maybe you two better come into the kitchen and sit down."

"We brought a few housewarming gifts. We weren't planning on crashing any parties. We just...care and want you to know," Bill said as he lifted the bags up, looking at her as though to gauge her reaction to their presence.

It was a relief and a help, and it made her feel less alone, but it also made her feel like they needed to leave so she could start living and making sure she could do this new life thing on her own.

That didn't make any sense, but she didn't know how else to explain it. She wanted to be sure she was able to stand on her own two feet. It felt like she'd been dependent on her husband and maybe even on her daughter for so long that she wasn't sure how to be alone.

The idea was scary and made her want to run back to the life that she left behind. The only problem was, that life was no longer there. Her husband, her ex-husband married someone else, and they had a child together. She was pregnant by another man, and her daughter was in LA, doing only who knew what, angry at the world, and rightfully so since her homelife had imploded and left her searching for answers that Kim didn't know how to give her.

"I appreciate your thoughtfulness," she said as she led Bev and Bill to the kitchen. "I actually just walked in the door and have done little more than look around. I...can't really give you a tour, unless you consider me exploring the house a tour."

"No. We didn't come for that today. After you get settled, maybe we can set up a time, and we'll bring food and we'll have supper and you can tell us about the house and how you're settling in." Bev set her bags of groceries on the counter, then turned and put arms around Kim.

They weren't quite like Iva May's arms, but they made her feel thirty years younger than what she was, and she laid her head on Bev's shoulder and wrapped her arms around her.

Life was scary, she didn't have health insurance, she barely had a home, she just kicked someone out in order to have a place to sleep, and she didn't know what kind of life she was going to bring her baby into.

For not the first time, she wondered if she should put her child up for adoption. She certainly wasn't in any shape to be raising a child. Financial or mental.

"That man was the father." The words slipped out as she stood in Bev's embrace.

She felt Bev still and tense under her.

"Davis?" Bill said, shock lacing the two syllables as they hung in the air.

"Yes. I don't know what he was doing here, I... I wasn't expecting him at all. But I didn't want you to not know."

"Does he know?" Bill asked low and slow.

Bev gave him a glance, which Kim interpreted to mean just relax and let her talk.

She almost laughed. Bill was the least pushy man she knew.

"No. I was just opening my mouth to tell him. Literally I had my mouth open, I just didn't know how to get the words out, when you knocked on the door."

"I'm sorry. That was terrible timing." Bev shook her head. "We should have stopped at that diner and eaten breakfast on the way out." She looked at Bill. "I told you we should."

"You're right as usual, my dear," Bill said, making Kim smile at his conciliatory and humble tone.

Bev chuckled and shook her head. "You don't have to agree with everything I say."

"Yes, dear."

They laughed together, and Kim couldn't help but smile. Her life might seem like it was falling apart, but she did have these two people who were really beautiful human beings in her corner. She knew she could ask them for anything, and they would do whatever they could to help her no matter what.

"That seems a little bit odd. That he would be here," Bill said, and all traces of humor were gone from his voice.

"I know. I just feel so confused and mixed up and like I'm not even sure how to figure out my life, let alone to begin to process that Davis is here."

"He seemed like a good man. Of course, men can hide a lot of things behind a humble exterior, but his humility really struck me."

"I don't know how someone can be so confident and so humble at the same time." Kim couldn't disagree. He did seem humble. Just an understated way of moving and talking that seemed respectful yet confident at the same time. She'd never really seen that mix in too many people and found it intriguing and attractive in Davis.

"I don't know if we're qualified to give you any advice, and I don't know if you'd want any, but we're definitely qualified to listen if you ever need to talk." Bev had stepped back but kept an arm around her, while Bill came from the other side and she felt safe between the two of them.

This was what having parents felt like. Two people in a person's corner who were always fighting for them. Always supporting them. Always there for them.

She supposed that was in an ideal situation. But how many of those ideal situations were there in the world anymore? Not many, she supposed.

"All right. We weren't going to stay, just wanted to drop off some staples—ketchup, mustard, butter, salt, and pepper. Things like that." Bev smiled and squeezed her waist. "We just want you to know that we love you."

"Thanks."

"And when you're ready to start fixing up the stable, if you need any help with the house, if you want someone to go to appointments with you, let us know. We don't know much, but we know people who do. And we're happy to help however we can."

"I appreciate it. Thank you. For everything." She couldn't quite get herself to say mom and dad, but in her heart, it felt like the words were there. Maybe next time.

They nodded and then slipped out the door.

Silence surrounded her, and she was grateful to have the peace and quiet for a bit where she could just sit and rest. She just needed time to think, time to plan, time to figure out what in the world she was going to do. But first, after she put the groceries away, she should take a walk through the house, familiarizing herself with it.

And then she needed to figure out what she was going to do about Davis; she couldn't put off telling him indefinitely, and although she dreaded it, she knew it was something that she had to do. The sooner the better. Maybe that's what she'd do as soon as she put the groceries away and took a tour of the house. She'd get that task out of the way, and then she could move on with her life.

Chapter 5

Davis stood in the apartment above the stable.

It wasn't a terrible apartment. There was a small bed, a kitchenette, and a shower and toilet in the tiny bathroom.

It was clean, and he appreciated that more than anything. He supposed after being rather successful in the business world, he'd gotten used to, if not living in the lap of luxury, at least having pretty much anything he wanted.

Material things. Since wanting people and having them wasn't quite as easy as wanting things.

He had admired Kim from the time he met her, but because she was married, he hadn't pursued her. Now... She didn't seem interested.

He hadn't missed the way she'd stumbled over introducing her parents, and he wondered about that. There was so much about her that he didn't know. But he knew divorce was hard, painful, it tore at a person's soul, and Kim was surely still reeling from that, not to mention it couldn't be easy when a person's ex, who had been the one to cheat, was the one who seemed like they bounced back and were thriving now that they were away from her.

That had to be hard too.

Still, being close to her was better than not. Although he couldn't quite put his finger on what exactly he felt and why he was going to such lengths.

He probably should just admit that his plan had been ill-conceived and pack up and go home.

Except the idea held no appeal. And more than just seeing Kim, being on the beach of Lake Michigan had been good for his soul. Soothing it, releasing stress, and helping him to open his eyes and actually see his life for the first time in a really long time.

Open his eyes and see how God might see his life.

There was no doubt being so close to such power and natural beauty couldn't help but point a person to their Creator.

He wasn't sure of what his next move would be, but he decided he'd change his clothes and go for a jog. That often helped clear his mind.

Lord? I thought I belonged here. And now I'm not so sure. Maybe I'm just getting in Kim's way. Maybe I'll just stunt her healing process. Maybe what I want isn't what I should be going after, maybe I should back off and allow her to find her way.

He didn't know the right answer, and he asked God to give him clarity.

He had just come out of his room when there was a knock at the door.

The door was solid wood, with nothing in it, not even a peephole, and he couldn't see who might be on the other side.

He also couldn't stop the way his heart kicked up in anticipation, and he knew exactly who he hoped it was.

Opening the door, he kept a huge smile from spreading across his face only by concentrating on trying not to scare her away. Kim stood there, looking determined yet wringing her hands in front of her while she looked like what she had come to do was not something she was looking forward to.

Maybe she decided that he couldn't live beside her after all. Maybe she decided that he needed to leave, and she was going to tell him.

There was definitely a sinking in the pit of his stomach, and his chest grew cold, but he remembered his prayer.

Lord, if she wants me to go, please, give me the strength to do it without argument, submitting to Your will.

"Davis?"

"Come on in, Kim. I…" He didn't know what to say around her. The night they spent together, they'd done more dancing, and other things, than talking, but he felt an ease with her that he'd never felt with anyone else. She seemed to fit perfectly in his arms, seemed to belong beside him. The talking they had done had felt exactly right. Their silences perfect, not awkward or uncomfortable.

It sounded cheesy, but that night, he felt like he found his soulmate.

He only regretted what came after, which was all his fault. He...should have known better. But it was heady to have Kim in his arms, and he'd made one stupid decision after another.

He should ask for her forgiveness. He wanted it. Wanted to start out with a clean slate, courting her the way she deserved and not treating her like she was only worth one night.

He wanted her for the rest of his life or at least wanted to see if that would be possible.

She came slowly in, and he closed the door behind her while she stopped in the middle of the room, seeming uncertain.

"I'm sorry there's not much. There's a couple of chairs in the kitchen and...not much else." There was one recliner in the small room that passed as the living room/dining room/sitting room.

But it would be awkward for her to be sitting while he stood, or vice versa.

"Maybe I'll just stand," she said, seeming to square her shoulders as she lifted her head and looked at him.

He had to be careful because just like all the clichés, he could get lost in her eyes.

"I'm pregnant. She's yours."

That's all she said. It was enough.

His lungs froze, while his heart seemed to fall out of his chest. His fingers tingled, and his knees felt like they were going to buckle.

"You're pregnant?" he repeated, his words echoing hers and not as much a question as just the words rolling around in his head and tumbling out of his mouth.

Kim. His baby. Them. Together. Parents. Her. Kim had said her. A daughter.

He didn't know when his mouth became dry, his throat tight, the back of his neck feeling stretched and taut, his body stiff like he couldn't move.

She nodded, her face dead serious. He hadn't imagined this, hadn't even considered.

He should have. Of course he should have. He was old enough to know better. But he didn't typically do those kinds of things, and he knew without a shadow of doubt that Kim didn't either.

Funny how people who do things like that all the time never got "caught." They were too smart and savvy. It was the people who hardly ever did it, the ones who had moral reasons for not, who were caught unprepared.

Like a teenager who should have known better but didn't think it could happen to them.

He supposed becoming a father without getting married first was a terrible thing at any age, but at his... It was embarrassing.

Except, was it terrible that there was a small part of him that was also thrilled? That was silently jumping for joy somewhere deep inside of him. That wanted to grab Kim, throw his arms around her, lift her up in the air, and smile and celebrate.

A new life. One they had made together.

"Am I allowed to be happy about that?" he finally said, realizing that beyond the shame and guilt, the knowing that he had done something he shouldn't have, beyond the embarrassment of anyone in the world who would say that he should have known better, used protection, should have made better decisions, beyond all that, his happiness was almost overwhelming.

"You can feel however you want to about it. I'm not sure how I feel." She put her arms around her stomach and turned away from him. He wanted to grab her, turn her back, promise her that everything was going to be okay, that they would raise the child together, that this would be the most loved child in the history of the world. That he wasn't going to let anything happen to her. That they could build a life for her together. The two of them. And then three. Maybe there'd even be a sibling.

He thought about his age, calculated how old he would be with their children graduated from high school, and decided that yes. He'd love that. Love to do that. He wasn't too old.

Family vacations. Suppers around the table. All the things that he didn't have growing up but wanted so badly, so fiercely. He wanted to give those to his child.

But the woman in front of him didn't look the slightest bit interested or welcoming.

"Maybe it will take some time for you to decide what you want?"

She nodded, her head jerking up and down in quick little shakes, making him feel like not only was she nervous, but she was scared too.

The desire to put his arms around her never left.

But he had gone too fast the last time. He had pulled her into his arms, and she swept him off his feet. Or maybe, maybe she had just wanted to lose herself somewhere, somehow, to dull the pain. Maybe she was still in love with her ex.

But that baby was his. He had rights. And the fact that she had told him, had made a special trip over and climbed the stairs above the stable just to tell him, made him feel that maybe she wanted him to be a part of it.

"Why did you tell me?"

"Why did I tell you?" She turned slightly, looking over her shoulder at him.

"Yeah."

"Don't you mean, why did it take me so long? Aren't you going to ask that? I've known for five months."

"You knew it at Iva May's funeral."

"I did."

"But I went with your ex."

"Right. And his new wife."

"They got married the day he signed the papers."

"I figured as much."

It wasn't hard to tell that that hurt her. That made him feel that she wasn't over Todd. The thought sliced deep, and he almost put a hand over his chest where the pain pinched hard.

"Do you still love him?" He couldn't help the words as they came out. Everything he wanted hinged on the fact that she wanted a new life. Something different. Of course, he was Todd's business partner, and maybe she wanted a break from everything that had to do with Todd, including him. But he hoped not.

"No. I... I guess I long for what might have been. When I said vows, I didn't mean to break them. I didn't mean to watch my husband walk away. To be with someone else. I... I meant for that to be my lifetime love. Forever and ever."

"I don't think anyone ever says vows thinking that they're not going to keep them. At least we shouldn't. I certainly understand the fight you had." He didn't know how to comfort her, didn't know what to say to make it better. "I want to be a dad."

That was a total change of subject, but if she wasn't still in love with Todd, if she wanted to move forward, there was hope. But he wasn't going to do it in a slapdash way. He'd messed up once. He couldn't go back and fix it, couldn't escape the consequences, if he even wanted to, but he could learn from his mistakes and do better this time.

Beginning with an apology.

"I'm sorry. I'm sorry for what happened that night. I'm sorry... Okay. I'm not sorry about what happened. I... It was a beautiful night. Everything was perfect. Except for the fact that...it was wrong. I'm sorry I didn't give you the respect you deserved, took something from you that wasn't mine to take."

It was a terrible apology. Terrible. But he didn't want her to think that he didn't love everything about that night, except the sin, what it said about how he valued her, and the guilt that had been eating at him ever since.

"I'm sorry that you have the consequences to deal with. I can't help you right now, but when she's here, I want to. I want to be a dad."

It hadn't taken him long at all to go from never expecting to have children to wanting with his whole heart and soul to make the world a beautiful place for his daughter. Hopefully, for his daughter and her mother. His wife.

That was definitely getting the cart ahead of the horse. He had to focus on Kim and what he could do to prove to her that what he had just said was true. He was sorry for not respecting her like she deserved but wasn't sorry for the amazing memories he had.

Chapter 6

"**Y**ou don't owe me any apologies." Kim took a breath, and her hand seemed to tighten around her middle as she turned back toward Davis. "It was my fault just as much as yours. I... I don't typically do things like that. I...just wasn't thinking, or maybe I wanted revenge. I don't know. I was being stupid. Sorry."

He stood straight, but her words hurt. There was no concession to any kind of feelings for him. It was all regret. She called her actions stupid.

He tried not to dwell on it, didn't want to nitpick her words apart. Didn't want to read more than what was there. Tried to remind himself that the way he acted in his circumstances was more important than the circumstances themselves. Whatever happened, he was here with Kim. He needed to be a man of character. Someone she might possibly be interested in doing more than co-parenting with.

"Are you going to allow me to help raise her?" He phrased the question like that, because he wanted to demand his parental rights. Demand that he was going to get their child, but she hadn't even had to tell him about her. He would never have known. Wouldn't have guessed. Except...now that they lived close together and he would have seen that she was pregnant, couldn't believe he missed it to begin with, and he would have wondered if he was the father.

"Did you only tell me because I was going to figure it out?"

"No!" she said immediately, her brows lifting, her eyes open and honest. "I... I honestly knew I needed to and planned to eventually, but so much has been happening. The divorce, the bad decisions, my daughter, losing my mom, having no place to land. Finding out that..." Whatever she was going to say, she cut off abruptly. "I really was going to tell you. I knew I needed to, I just hadn't gotten my life straightened out enough to figure out how. Or what, or even what that would look like."

"We have three months. Right?"

She nodded.

Unless the baby came early.

"Is everything all right?" His words were soft, with as much caring and gentleness as he could put in them. Wanting her to know that he was truly concerned, that he truly did care.

"My age puts me at high risk." Her cheeks pinkened a little. Like it was uncomfortable to think of herself as anything but young. He certainly knew the feeling. He was looking hard at forty. Twenty years ago, forty had seemed like over the hill and through the woods with one foot in the grave. But now, he didn't feel like that at all when he thought about his age.

"But the doctors have said that everything has been perfect. I'll... I'll continue going to the hospital in Blueberry Beach. It's not that far away, just thirty minutes. And hopefully everything will continue to go well."

"How have you been feeling?" He had a million questions he wanted to ask. So many things he wanted to know. Had she had an ultrasound? Were there pictures of his baby? What was she going to name her? And he had questions about Kim too. What did she want from him?

What was she expecting? What would be best for her? He hadn't been there to feel the baby move, to share the excitement of finding out about a new life. Although, it probably wasn't exciting to her. It was probably...devastating.

"We can make this a good thing, right?"

"I wasn't even sure I was going to keep her." She sounded like she was admitting something she didn't want to.

"I will. Please. Let me."

Her lips flattened, but maybe there was a little bit of relief in her gaze as well. "I guess you don't have to worry about where your next meal is coming from."

"Neither do you. I promise. You don't have to worry about anything that has to do with money."

She shook her head. "That was part of the reason I hesitated to tell you. I didn't want anyone to say that I was after you for money. I don't want a dime."

He admired her spirit. And he didn't blame her. Not really. She didn't have much of anything left. When that happened, a person had a tendency to pull the things that they did have tightly around them and hold them fast as though fending off the rest of the world. But he had time to break through the wall she'd constructed around herself. Or maybe, he had time to chip away at it, carefully removing pieces until she allowed him to stand before her without the wall between them.

He liked the picture that presented, because he liked the idea of wooing her, of gently courting her, of treating her the way she deserved to be treated.

Todd certainly hadn't done that. It had made Davis angry more than once when he'd seen the way Todd neglected and disregarded his wife.

She deserved so much more.

"Yes. Whatever I do, I want you to be involved too. I guess I just don't know what that is. And if you don't mind giving me some time."

"I don't mind at all. If you don't mind me living here?"

She bit her lip and looked around. "I feel terrible about this. But I don't know what else to do? I don't have anywhere to go."

"Right now, I don't either." And that wasn't entirely untrue. He did have several other places, but they weren't ready for him. Of course, he could make a phone call and have them ready the next day, but he didn't elaborate. He wanted to be here. Maybe he should say that.

"After I've spent just a few months here in Strawberry Sands, there's... There's something here that really fills my soul with things that I needed. Maybe it's emptied it of the things I didn't. And hopefully I'm slowly becoming a new, and better, man. I need to stay." There. That was the truth.

She nodded. "Maybe there will be a place in town that will open up." She sighed. "But it bothers me that you signed a lease with my mom. I need to honor it."

"I understand why you wouldn't want us living together. That...doesn't look very good. And it's not something I've ever done."

"Me, either."

But her expression still looked worried. She swallowed.

Part of him wanted to demand that she keep her mother's word since that would put them in even closer proximity, but he didn't want to push her harder than she could handle and demand more of her than she was ready to give.

"I… I suppose a marriage of convenience, I've heard of them, just a business arrangement which would allow you to live in the house and ease both of our consciences—"

"No. I'm fine out here. This is still part of your mother's property, and so technically you're keeping her word." He understood that was a problem with her, and he wanted to ease her mind about that. He knew there were people who didn't care whether or not they kept the details of a contract and would get away with whatever they could get away with. He appreciated the fact that Kim wasn't like that.

He hoped, someday, he'd be able to tell her how tempting the offer was to have a marriage of convenience. At least to be married to her would be half the battle. Maybe three quarters.

But he'd already done things the easy, quick way six months previous, and if he'd learned anything, it was that easy and quick didn't really work in relationships. Not for him anyway. He needed more time, he wanted Kim not to marry him because of convenience, but because she wanted to. Because she loved him.

"Of course. I know you wouldn't be interested in marriage, that's just the only way..."

"I understand. And it's not that I'm not interested, it's that I already got the cart ahead of the horse. I don't want to do that again. I want to have a good relationship with you. You're the mother of my child, and I think it's important that we get along."

He wanted to say a lot more. That he wanted the relationship to grow, to develop into something deeper, solid and strong. A lifetime relationship. One that included love and most definitely included marriage and everything that entailed, but it was obvious that Kim was just getting her sea legs, and he didn't want to push her. He wanted to help her. And that meant shoving back the things that he wanted, focusing on her. After all, it had been shocking to know that he was going to be a father, but he hadn't just lost his mom, hadn't just gone through a bitter divorce, hadn't found out that the woman who raised him wasn't his actual mother, hadn't just moved to an entirely new community. All of those things were things that would upend someone's life. But to go through them all in such a short time, no wonder she was confused.

"Do you want me to help you carry your things in?" he asked, trying to figure out what he could do to start working toward his goal of helping her and developing a relationship with her.

"No. I don't have that much. I sold a lot. I guess I did a lot of cleaning, both in my life and in reality."

"Kim?"

Her brows went up, and she blinked, as though she needed to pull herself out of her thoughts.

"I just wanted you to know that I'm here if you need me."

"Thanks. I'll try not to bother you. I'm sure you'll be working."

"Didn't Todd tell you?" He shook his head. Of course he didn't tell her. Todd probably wasn't talking to her at all. "He bought out my half of the business."

She didn't have much of a reaction, just a jerk of her head, and then maybe a thoughtful look crossed her face. Maybe she wondered if that was why her marriage settlement had been so low.

Todd had bragged to everyone about how much he had paid her and how she didn't deserve it. Davis supposed Todd was trying to make himself look generous and benevolent and get people's minds off the idea that Kim deserved every penny she had gotten for putting up with the likes of him and because he had cheated.

"So what are you doing?" Kim asked, tilting her head like the idea had just occurred to her that he might be starting over as she had.

"I had a few things already in the fire. Things I can do from wherever I'm at. Things that don't really take a lot of time. I guess you talked about doing some cleaning in your life as well as in your reality, and I suppose I was doing the same. It started...a little bit before you and I..." He wasn't sure what to say about that night. What to call it. How to refer to it. He regretted it because it was wrong, but he didn't regret the time he'd spent with her. Couldn't refer to it as a mistake or in any negative way, other than wishing he had been stronger in character.

She shook her head. "You don't have to mince words because of me. Trust me, I'd take it back if I could."

He wasn't sure if that meant she regretted what she did with him, or she regretted their baby, or both, everything. Maybe someday he'd find out.

"Anyway, I will have to do some work here, but there is a rumor going around in town that someone was going to open up the stable again. I used to have horses when I was a kid, and I really enjoyed them. I think that would go perfectly with the way my life is turning out." He laughed a little. "I suppose some men have a midlife crisis and they do all kinds of crazy things, I suppose selling a multimillion-dollar business and becoming the manager of a beach riding stable that, at this point, is nonexistent probably qualifies me to land on the crazier side of loony."

"Or maybe you just discovered what you don't want and are looking for something that you do."

"I just think that maybe God might have a use for me here. I've lived my life mostly for me so far. I think Strawberry Sands is the place where I change that."

"At least it's not a jungle in South America."

"God's been good. What can I say?" He lifted his shoulder and gave her, not his charming smile, but a real grin, one that he hoped was friendly but also showed that he was serious about wanting to do what God wanted him to do. There wasn't much doubt in his mind, if any, that Strawberry Sands was where he was supposed to be. There was just such a peace about the place and a feeling of rightness he felt every time he thought of putting down roots here.

"If you'd like, I can show you around town." He hadn't meant to offer that.

Hadn't even thought that might be something she would like, but he was glad the words came out. "It's small, a little run down, maybe you've seen it?"

"No. I haven't. I was hoping that there would be a diner. I'm hungry and tired. I don't feel like cooking."

"That's pretty much me all the time. There isn't much in the way of groceries there. But it looked to me like your parents... Your parents?"

She nodded but didn't say anything else. Maybe someday she would open up to him about the things that went on in her head. And her heart.

He didn't typically go around wanting to know what anyone was thinking or feeling, but with Kim, the thoughts came unbidden. And he found himself wanting more than just the surface interaction. He wanted something deeper.

"I don't want to put you out."

"It would be an honor, but I don't want to push in if you prefer to spend some time alone. I know what it's like to need to regroup."

She looked interested. "You do?"

"There is a diner in town, and if you let me pay for your supper, I'll tell you about my regrouping. It probably wasn't quite as dramatic as yours, but it was traumatic for me at the time."

She bit her lips, pulling them both in and nodding as she looked away from him, back at the brown wainscoting that lined the wall of the small room where they stood.

Finally she said, "I guess it would be a good idea for us to get to know each other. I..." She put a hand up as though warding him off. "I'm not looking for any-thing more. But for the sake of our child, we need to be...friends maybe? There's a huge part of me that wants to be alone, but there is another, maybe even big-ger part of me that's scared. And wants some company."

"I know you know that there's no need to be scared. Whatever is happening isn't going to be a surprise to the Lord."

"I know. I keep thinking that."

"And a lot of times, circumstances that look terrifying aren't really what they seem. And I can tell you from experience that when you feel like you hit the bottom, a lot of times you bounce. You end up in a better spot than what you were when you started to fall."

"That's encouraging. I'd really like to bounce. I guess it could be a goal."

"A lot of times, it's the way you look at things that starts to shift your opinion and your thoughts and helps you see that things aren't quite as bleak as what they seem."

"You know, maybe eating with you is a good idea, because I like what you're saying. It's exactly what I need to hear. I know it's true."

"You're going to give me a big head. And maybe instead of being your stable manager, I'll start charging you for counseling."

She gave a wan smile, like maybe she couldn't quite joke about the idea of having counseling just yet. "I went to the counselor for a few sessions, but they just told me what I wanted to hear, instead of telling me the hard things. Maybe I'm just a sucker for punishment, but I didn't want to hear all of the easy stuff. I wanted to be challenged. That's what I need to get myself dug out of the hole. To put my eyes on Jesus and start working."

"That's the best attitude. Come on, I'll take you into town and show you around. We can't wait too long, because Strawberry Sands is not exactly a hip place, and pretty much everything closes by six or seven o'clock in the evening."

"Even in the summer?"

"I haven't been here that long, but you're probably right. Things probably stay open longer when the beach is busy." He opened the door, and she walked out ahead of him.

Now that he knew what he did, he could see the slight shuffle in her walk, the way her shirt ebbed and flowed, concealing her stomach. He was no expert on pregnant women and really had no idea of how big the baby would be or how big he should expect her to be, but she seemed small.

He'd already asked about the baby's health, and she might be offended if he phrased another question about whether the baby was growing properly or not. Maybe taking her to eat would have a second benefit, and that would be that she would actually eat. Maybe she hadn't been. Not that he could blame her. She'd been through so much. As much as possible, he vowed to make things as easy for her as he could from here on out.

Chapter 7

This was not how Kim planned to spend the evening.

She'd arrived sad and depressed, just wanting to be alone.

She could hardly believe how the Lord had worked things out. Davis in her home, his offer to live above the stable, her parents coming with housewarming gifts that warmed her heart, and now? She was going out to eat with the father of her baby.

Life sure took crazy turns sometimes.

Thank you, Lord. You definitely got my mind off of myself and onto other things. Maybe that's what I needed, when I thought what I needed was to sit at the cottage and pity myself. You saw that I needed more.

She supposed she shouldn't be surprised that God knew exactly what she needed and sent it to her, but she kind of was.

She didn't exactly feel happy, but there was definitely joy poking out of her soul. Maybe if she fanned the flames, that joy would turn into a full-fledged joy down in her heart.

A joy that oozed out of every pore and made her smile over nothing.

That was the kind of person she used to be. Back before her husband had cheated and her daughter had gone astray and her mom had cancer and her aunt had taken the home that she was supposed to inherit right out from underneath her.

Her step felt lighter, her breath easier, as she stopped as they stepped out of the stable, and she lifted her head toward the lake. She breathed deeply, good, fresh, clean air, air that smelled like pure water, with just a nip of cold in it. Just enough to make her feel clean and rejuvenated.

It wasn't the stagnant, still, stench-filled air of water in a warmer climate. But bracing and wild and perfect.

"It's getting a hold of you too, isn't it?" Davis said from beside her, and she startled a bit, because she honestly had completely forgotten about him. Which was hard to believe, since his presence commanded her every nerve.

"I think it is."

"Imagine how that would feel from horseback."

"It's like a dream come true. Do you really think we could make a go of that kind of business?"

He nodded. "Folks from Blueberry Beach would travel the whole way up here to rent horses. I'm sure of it, because there is a family just up the beach who has a small stable as well."

That made her heart sink, instead of making her happy. "Maybe they don't need a second one?"

"I've actually talked to Matt Landry, his family owns the riding stable up the beach." Davis looked confident, and that eased Kim's heart somewhat. "They have about ten horses, and throughout the summer, all ten of them are completely booked. He gives them at least one day off a week where they have no rides booked, but he said they often are booked for a ride in the morning and one in the afternoon. He recommended that's what we start with, which sounded good to me. I... I don't mean to tell you what to do."

"No. You're not. And I respect your business sense." Her voice trailed off a little, although she didn't mean for it to. But she was thinking about him being in business with her husband. There was no doubt that their business had been successful.

"I don't want you to think that because I was in business with your husband, I'm like him." He spoke like he could read her mind, and maybe that's because her thoughts were reflected on her face, but he sounded concerned and sincere.

The wind blew Kim's hair across her face, and she reached up and tucked it behind her ear. "I know you're different. I heard him complaining more than once that he wanted to do something that would make a lot of money and you refused because it was unethical. I know that's crazy, but it made me respect you. Every time you defied him to do what was right, he would growl and be angry, which wasn't pleasant, but even before I met you, I really, really liked you."

She felt her cheeks getting hot, and she turned her face to the wind, ostensibly to look out over the lake and feel the breeze. Not to hide her heating cheeks and the embarrassment over what she had just said. Obviously she liked him, after the night they'd had together, he could hardly doubt it, but that wasn't the kind of like she meant.

"I don't know how to make it so that night isn't sitting between us, but I wish it wasn't."

Her effort to hide her embarrassment apparently did not work. He could tell exactly what she was thinking and somehow figured out the source of her embarrassment.

"I wish it wasn't either."

"We can't change it, so let's just acknowledge that we...did something completely out of character for both of us, and maybe just move on?"

That wasn't quite what she wanted to hear. Aside from the fact that she couldn't just erase the knowledge of that night from her brain, his gentleness, his care, how cherished she felt, the way she fit perfectly in his arms. She didn't really want to erase any of it.

She liked the fact that earlier he said that he didn't regret it other than the sin and guilt. That was pretty much how she felt too, but she wasn't sure how she felt about having a baby at her age, unwed, with no job, having just lost her mother and with her only other daughter turning her back on everything she'd been raised to be.

She loved Alyssa, but it was discouraging. It made having another baby less exciting and more like she was filled with dread because she might screw up again.

"Yeah. Let's move on. I... I probably will have a little bit of trouble, because I'm embarrassed. But I think you're right. Let's just start fresh. We can be friends. We can co-parent. We can do this." She looked up at him, some of the joy that she'd been feeling since he gave her his little pep talk up in his living room coming back.

God was there. He wasn't surprised. He already knew the way, and He would hold her hand with every step she took. That was encouraging and reassuring, and she wanted to hold on to those promises.

"Come on. I'm hungry."

To her surprise, she found that she was actually feeling a little hungry too. Hunger had been something she hadn't felt much of in the last few months. Too many other things stealing her thoughts and subduing her appetite.

"Would you like to walk?" Davis asked as he stepped around his truck, his hand on the passenger door, as though he were going to open it up for her if she wanted.

"Sure. I appreciate that."

He smiled at her, and she smiled back, and for some reason, she felt like maybe they'd just come to an understanding. Maybe they really had moved past that night, and they were going to start building something new, something on a stronger foundation, something that would withstand the test of time.

Chapter 8

Charlotte wiped the table and tried not to question her life choices. Choices that had led her to open a diner in the almost dead lakeside town of Strawberry Sands.

She'd given it the original title of Beachside Bakery, and she had a lot of high hopes when she opened.

Those high hopes had dwindled to a little bit of nothing. The idea that maybe she could make it for at least a year so she didn't go running home with her tail between her legs, embarrassed that her lifelong dream of owning a bakery had crashed and burned so quickly, almost seemed like too much to ask. She'd be lucky if they made it another month.

The bell over the door jangled, and Davis Thatcher, a newer resident of Strawberry Sands from what she understood, although he had been there longer than she had, came in with a woman she didn't recognize.

As the owner of the local eatery, the only one in town, Charlotte knew pretty much everyone.

"Hello, it's a beautiful day," Charlotte said, knowing her words were true, even if they didn't match the spreading depression in her chest. "Seat yourself and I'll be over, okay, Davis?" She nodded her head at the woman beside Davis, who nodded back in greeting with a curious look between the two of them.

There was nothing going on there. Chi didn't have time for romance, even though Davis was rather good looking, if she looked at him objectively.

But she finally got her life turned around, and she wasn't going to derail it over an ill-conceived romance.

Plus, it looked like he had someone. The woman with him was probably considered tall in some circles, although her head only came to Davis's shoulder. She looked a little chunky too, to Charlotte's trained eye. She worked in the fashion industry for a while; of course, she worked at a lot of jobs for a while. It looked like she was going to work at owning a diner for a while too, before she fell into something else.

Of course, since she changed the way she lived, she didn't have as many options open to her.

Throwing the rag behind the counter, she grabbed two menus and her notepad and walked over to the booth where Davis and the woman had settled themselves.

"I'm Charlotte," she said to the woman who looked up as she approached.

"I'm Kim," the woman said, meeting her eyes, as Charlotte put the menus down on the table in front of them. "I like your choice of music," Kim added.

Chi grinned, appreciating that the woman had noticed that she was playing hymn music over the speakers. She always had some kind of hymns playing, and strings were her favorite. Maybe that accounted for the lack of popularity of her restaurant.

Of course, a lack of customers might also be because Strawberry Sands wasn't exactly the bustling beach town she had been expecting when she bought it.

At least the bustling beach town hadn't materialized yet.

"Thanks. I like to have something playing that reminds me of the direction I want to live my life."

Kim nodded thoughtfully. "That's a great idea."

Charlotte might be imagining things, but Davis seemed to look at Kim like she hung the moon and stars. Interesting, because she hadn't pictured Davis as anything other than confident and successful.

He was dressed like he was about to take a jog, so he wasn't exactly screaming businessman today, nor did it say he was trying to impress a woman, but the way he looked at Kim was interesting.

"Can I take your drink orders?" Charlotte asked, pulling her pen and pad out. She wouldn't have any trouble remembering, since there weren't any other customers in the diner, but it was a habit.

They each gave her their drink orders, and she said, like she did every time, "I have some bakery goods in the case; you can go look at them, or I can bring you a list of what we have today. Griff and I made everything fresh this morning."

"And everything I've ever had here is absolutely amazing. Except for the shoofly pie." Davis gave an exaggerated shudder.

"True, but in my defense, you'd never had shoofly pie, and it's really not for everyone."

"I'm not saying it wasn't well-made, I'm just saying I didn't particularly enjoy it."

"Have you ever had shoofly pie?" Charlotte asked Kim, figuring that she'd give her a piece on the house if she hadn't.

"Is that like mincemeat?" Kim asked, crinkling her brows.

"No. Mincemeat is a completely different thing. But we do have that occasionally as well."

"I like mincemeat. At least the one time I had it. I've never made it myself."

"I'll get you a piece of shoofly. It's molasses based, and if you don't like molasses, then you probably won't like it."

"I'm not sure if I've ever had molasses. Although aren't there Christmas cookies made of molasses?"

They chatted a bit about it, then Charlotte left to grab their drinks and to slice off a small piece of shoofly pie for Kim to try.

She liked the way Davis looked at and treated Kim, and she was curious as to what exactly was going on.

Maybe that's what made her a good diner owner, because even though Strawberry Sands was small, and her diner was struggling, and she wasn't sure whether she was even going to make it to the next month, let alone for an entire year, she loved the people in the town and cared about them.

It was one of those small towns where everyone knew everyone else and everyone cared about everyone else. It was exactly the kind of place that she needed to land after all the poor choices she'd made in her life.

There were lots of people she could blame for how her life ended up, but she always found it best when she took the blame for herself.

And now she had the eye of a great man, handsome and upstanding, a lawyer in Chicago who had a big beach house nearby and who had come into her diner to eat a few times. They'd hit it off, and he texted her once in a while. She had every expectation that they'd develop a great relationship and maybe progress to more. She hoped so.

She grabbed the drinks and the slice of pie, shoved her notebook in her pocket, and walked back over to their table.

After setting the drinks down, she set the pie down and said, "It won't hurt my feelings either way. But people who love molasses usually really love the pie."

"Thanks so much. I appreciate the opportunity to taste it. I've never even heard of it before."

"I don't think it's something that's real common in this part of the country. I come from southern Ohio, and it's a much bigger thing there."

"Amish roots?" Davis asked, like he was familiar with the area.

She nodded. Not wanting to talk about it. She had moved away from that part of her life, and while she'd come back from the depths she traveled, she wasn't quite ready to go home.

She probably would never be ready to go home.

"I didn't want to introduce Kim without her permission, but she and I are expecting a baby in three months. She'll be here at Strawberry Sands. Her mom," he tripped over the word "mom," which Charlotte found odd, "owned the house I am leasing."

That was quite a bit of information. She certainly hadn't thought of Davis as the kind of man who had a woman running around who was pregnant. He hadn't said anything about her being his wife.

That was completely common in today's day and age, and Charlotte supposed she shouldn't be shocked. She certainly couldn't judge. Not with her past.

"Well, congratulations. Boy or girl?" she asked, having all day to talk. It wasn't like she was expecting a lunch or supper rush. Or any kind of rush for that matter.

"A girl," Kim said softly, sweetly.

Charlotte liked her and had a feeling that they could be friends. "Do you have names picked out?"

Kim's eyes went to Davis before she looked back at Charlotte. "No. Not yet. We have three months. I guess we'll have to figure something out eventually." She laughed a little nervously.

Charlotte took their orders, wondering about what was going on exactly. People had such interesting stories.

She tucked her notebook in her pocket, grabbed her tray, and assured them that she would be back out with their salads shortly.

Talk about interesting stories, she thought to herself as she walked into the kitchen where her short-order cook stood at the griddle, scraping its already clean surface.

Griff had heard people come in, and he'd turned the griddle on to get ready. She couldn't have found a better person to work for her, even if it had been an accident.

He'd shown up in town, tattoos covering both arms, bandanna around his head, two earrings in his left ear, wearing a leather vest, which exposed biceps bigger than her thighs and a thatch of chest hair that looked to be about as thick as the hair on her head sticking up from the V in his vest, worn jeans, and biker boots, his Harley parked along the sidewalk.

He had watched her walk down the sidewalk and use her key to open the door of the diner. Just a few minutes later, he'd knocked on the door and asked if she needed a short-order cook.

She couldn't deny that she needed one, and Griff turned out to be the cook of her dreams.

Well, the cook of her dreams didn't have quite that many tattoos and probably talked a little more too.

But Griff was good at his job. As much time as they spent together, she would have thought she would have gotten his story out of him. But he was very tight-lipped, and he knew way more about her than she knew about him.

Which wasn't saying much.

She handed him the order. He stuck it on the board above his head, and she didn't need to tell him that she would make the salads.

They worked together better than any-one Chi had ever worked with before, very seldom needing words. It was al-most like Griff read her mind, and some-how she was able to read his body lan-guage.

Regardless, someday she was going to get his story. Although, he was the kind of man who didn't stay in any place very long. After he started, she'd wondered pretty much every morning whether he was going to show up. So far, he had, but it wouldn't surprise her to open the diner some morning and find him gone, with no word and never hearing from him again. The idea made her sad. She got attached to people way too easily.

Of course, he rented the second apartment above the diner from her, so not only was he her employee, he was also her neighbor. No wonder she was attached.

To her surprise, when she walked back out with the salads, there were two more people sitting in a booth next to the front window.

Goodness, the place was just hopping. She almost went back into the kitchen to warn Griff. Or to tell him so they could celebrate together, she wasn't sure which. But Griff's idea of celebrating was probably to grunt a little louder than normal.

It didn't matter. She could celebrate for both of them. Hopefully, this was just the beginning of all the good things to come.

Chapter 9

Griff glanced up from the grill. He'd scraped it clean and could see out the window that there were no new customers.

Chi had been beaming about having more customers than normal, and seeing the excitement in her eyes made his heart swell.

He hadn't been meaning to stop in Strawberry Sands, had just wanted to spend a day or two in the small, non-commercialized town, enjoying the view of the lake and the freedom riding his bike offered. But from the first moment he'd seen the diner owner, there was just something about her that drew him, and he parked his bike, hung his keys up, and picked up a spatula.

He wasn't sure what it was about her, but all she had to do was look like she wanted something and it made him want to give it to her.

Unfortunately, all she saw was his outside, the tats and piercings, the gruff exterior, maybe even the boots and leather. His bike. She'd already written him off as someone she would never be interested in.

But she definitely chatted it up with that fancy lawyer from Chicago.

Griff could tell her that the lawyer had cheater written all over him. Funny how Chi couldn't seem to see it.

Still, when Chi had been in earlier, chatting about Kim and Davis and them opening a riding stable, it had made Griff realize that possibly he could be a help in this small town.

Hanging the spatula up on its hook, he wiped his hands on a dish towel from the counter and stepped around the island in the big industrial kitchen.

"Oh!" Chi said as she pushed through the door with dirty plates in her hand. "Are you quitting?" A wrinkle appeared between her eyes, worry crossing her face. She paused with her back against the door, her body half turned.

He wasn't quitting. Wouldn't think of it. She still needed him. He supposed he'd ride away when she was on her feet and married to the fancy lawyer, because that was coming. He was sure of it. Wasn't really what he wanted, but he was old enough to know that sometimes people didn't get what they wanted.

"I wanted to talk to Davis." He didn't owe her an explanation of what he was doing or where he was going, and most people wouldn't have gotten it, but Chi was the exception for a lot of things. Apparently.

"Oh," she said and visibly relaxed.

She stepped forward, keeping her heel by the door, holding it open for him.

He moved, her familiar scent almost making him hesitate, but he put one booted foot in front of the other, nodding at her before turning his eyes toward the counter area outside.

He knew Davis, although not well. They had spent a few evenings together at the diner, when Davis had been the only customer, and he'd sat at the counter, chatting through the window with Griff as he stood in the kitchen, nothing to do.

He didn't like to be idle, didn't like standing around, but he couldn't invent customers or work.

Still, it had given him some time to get to know Davis, who had seemed like a straight-up kind of guy, even if he was a businessman. Griff didn't trust those kinds of men. After all, he used to be one.

He walked to the table, his eyes on the couple. There was something between them. That much was obvious. He found, after he'd grown up a little, that when a person kept their mouth shut and their eyes open, they had a tendency to notice things that people who ran their mouth all the time didn't.

Definitely there was some tension under the surface between Davis and Kim. He bet there was some history there. A relationship.

But Chi hadn't said anything about them being married. Just that they were going into business together.

"I heard you're starting a riding stable?"

"You heard right," Davis said, standing up and offering his hand which Griff took and shook. "This is Kim. I don't think you probably met her, since she just arrived in Strawberry Sands today."

"Kim," Griff said, nodding at the woman who nodded back at him. She didn't get up to shake the hand he offered, taking it from her seat instead.

Davis settled himself back in his booth, and Griff said, "I know where there are some horses if you're interested."

"Really?" Kim said, her eyes widening with interest.

Davis seemed a little bit more reserved, but the openness of his face showed that he trusted Griff, which Griff appreciated.

"I have a buddy who doesn't live too far from here, who rescues horses from the kill pen."

"Kill pen?" Kim asked, looking confused.

"It's where they're sold as slaughter animals. Not for human consumption of course, but for slaughter nonetheless."

It was just a fact of life, not one he liked, necessarily, but one that he would not be able to change.

"My buddy looks for horses that maybe have been abused or that he feels still have potential."

"I see."

"They're usually very cheap. He takes them home, works with them."

"And he has some for sale?" Davis asked, pushing his drink around, absentmind-edly, like he was rolling all the business implications over in his head.

"He does. You can talk to him. I know he would have some that would work for you. Of course, not all the ones he has will work. I assume you're looking for horses good for beginners?"

"I think so?" Kim sounded uncertain, and she worried her lip with her teeth before glancing at Davis.

"I don't think that Kim has a business plan or anything like that, but maybe it's something we can talk about?" He looked to Kim whenever he spoke, and his words caused relief to flow over her face as she nodded.

Griff bit back a smile. It was obvious that Davis cared very deeply about Kim, and he would guess that Kim felt the same way, although she was a little harder for him to read, emotionally.

"If you guys want to go yourselves, I can give you the directions and just let him know you're coming. His name is George."

"That would be wonderful," Kim said immediately.

Davis pulled his phone out of his pocket, then leaned back in the booth seat. "How about you give me your number?"

"Sure." Griff pulled his own phone out, and they exchanged numbers.

He smiled to himself as he bid them farewell and turned to walk back to the kitchen. It felt like he was doing something good, not just helping them, but helping the horses too. It was a little bit the way he felt about working for Chi. Like he was doing something that was a little bit bigger than himself. Nothing huge, he wasn't saving the world or anything, he was just helping. It was much better than anything he'd done with the first part of his life.

As he turned, he noted that Chi had been standing a little ways away, a rag in her hand like she came out to wipe tables but stopped to listen. He would have invited her to go out with him to talk to them, but there was no reason. It wasn't like they were together, and it wasn't like she had anything to do with what Kim and Davis were doing.

He wished they were together.

Sometimes if a person was patient, things worked out better than what they thought they would. Griff didn't think this was one of those times, but he would continue to hope. Nodding at Chi, he walked on by, back into the kitchen.

Sometimes, instead of just waiting, a person could work toward what they wanted. He needed to think about that.

Chapter 10

Davis's step slowed as they got to the end of their driveway.

Kim pulled at the hem of her T-shirt, not sure what to say. Lunch had been delicious, but they hadn't talked about anything important, and the walk home had been quiet.

"I don't want you to feel like you have to help me," she finally said, thinking that maybe he'd only volunteered because he felt bad for her.

"I don't want to push myself in. But I'll do as much as you let me."

She twisted the hem of her T-shirt and then untwisted it before she said, "You're not pushing yourself in. But… I don't want to go into a partnership."

She actually wouldn't mind being in a partnership. It was scary to be all by herself.

Of course God was there. But sometimes she had a hard time remembering that, and the idea that everything was on her shoulders, all the work, all the responsibility, all the risk, made it hard to breathe at times.

"I was married, obviously, and that was enough partnership for me."

She didn't mean to sound bitter, but she'd trusted Todd, and he totally let her down. Never again. She would never again put herself in that position. Even while she thought that, there was a little voice whispering that maybe she just hadn't trusted the right person.

She didn't want to go there again. Even if it worked out the second time, she just...didn't have the energy to put into building a relationship that might or might not work out. She had no guarantee.

She wanted guarantees. She wanted to do things that were sure. But there wasn't much in life that was sure.

However, her business would have a much better chance of succeeding if

Davis was willing to help her. He had experience that she didn't and knew a lot of things that could help her.

"I know we're not talking about marriage, but I guess I just trusted people and got burned. I prefer not to have that happen again."

"I wasn't thinking of a partnership. Not really. I was just thinking of helping you however I can."

"Why?" She tilted her head and looked at him. That's what she didn't understand. Why he was here to begin with. Surely he knew that Iva May was her mother when he rented the house. Why? There were millions of houses in the state of Michigan, and lots were along the shores of

Lake Michigan. Why had he rented this one?

And why was he helping her now?

It just seemed too...coincidental for it to be for real.

"I don't think you're ready for the answer for that," he finally said, after staring at the horizon for several long minutes.

That didn't help at all, and she had no idea what that meant.

"But if you're willing to accept my help, I'm willing to give it. Want to."

"I'm willing. But I think I need a nap now. Could we...start tomorrow?"

"Let's do that. Do you know anything about the stable?"

"I haven't even been in it. Other than seeing you there today." She still felt bad that he was living above the stable, but there was no solution to that problem, other than her moving out or them getting married, neither of which was a viable solution for her.

"All right. Then let's plan on looking over what we have tomorrow morning, and then we'll sit down and draw up some ideas. Then, Sunday, if it suits Griff's friend George, we'll go see some horses. Does that sound good?"

"It does." She nodded decisively. He hadn't gotten offended when she stiff-armed him, making sure they kept the distance between them that she needed for them to have.

She appreciated that. Probably more than she could articulate even though she didn't really want there to be distance between them. Which totally contradicted everything she had been thinking, but it was the truth too.

She wished that wasn't so much a part of her makeup, but it was, sometimes wanting two totally contradictory things. She supposed maybe that was part of being a woman, because men didn't typically seem to have that problem, but she wasn't sure what to do about it. She didn't want to use her weakness as an excuse.

Davis walked her to her door, opening it before she had a chance to do it herself.

She tried not to be charmed, but she was. It was...unexpected and sweet. There hadn't been too much sweetness in her life, not from men.

"Thank you," she said, trying not to let him see how much he disarmed her by his gallant gesture. Surely she was too old to be influenced by a little bit of charm and a handsome man's attention.

"My pleasure," he said, and the words shivered down her backbone. She tried to push the feeling away. She didn't want shivery words, or surface charm, or a man's attention which only faded when he found something, or someone, newer and better.

She'd been there, she'd done that, and she wanted to do something different with the rest of her life.

Except... Davis was different.

"See you tomorrow," she said, putting her purse over her shoulder and walking into her house. She didn't invite him in and didn't turn to see if he went to the stable after he shut her door. She felt bad enough as it was. There were three bedrooms in her house, and she was just being stubborn by not letting him in. But she didn't want to go there. Didn't even want to give the appearance of evil. That's what the Bible said, and she had determined that she would live according to God's rules, not man's. Most of the people she knew would scoff at the idea of balking the way she was, but most of the people she knew didn't take the Bible seriously either.

She decided, after doing some research, that there truly was a God, and that He loved her and cared for her, and that He'd written the Bible.

If she believed that, if she believed that Jesus was the atonement for sin, the son of God sent as a sacrifice for all mankind, she couldn't continue to live like it didn't matter.

Maybe this new baby, she put her hand on her stomach as she put her purse on the table, maybe this new baby was her chance to do things over.

Thinking about that, she kicked her shoes off and dialed Alyssa's number.

She missed her daughter and wished there was something she could do for her. Even while she knew that like Kim, Alyssa was going to need to make her own mistakes. Unfortunately, Kim couldn't shake the idea that Alyssa was making mistakes that could have been avoided if Kim had avoided mistakes in her own life. Those were the worst mistakes to watch your child make. The ones that you knew were your fault.

Holding her phone to her ear, she settled on the couch, propping her feet up. Noting that her ankles were slightly swollen. Remembering how tired she had been with her first pregnancy and feeling that same bone-deep exhaustion.

The phone rang, and rang and rang, and she'd about given up on the idea Alyssa was going to answer when she heard a groggy voice on the other end of the line, "Hello?"

Not Alyssa's voice. It was a man.

"I was looking for my daughter."

"Hey. I think it's your mom." There was some murmuring on the other end of the line, and then the man said, "What's your daughter's name?"

She was irritated. She called her daughter, and now her daughter had a gatekeeper? She didn't even know this man. She wanted to demand his name, but that wasn't going to be the way to her daughter's good graces. She needed to be humble. After all, it wasn't like she'd never made mistakes.

So she spoke, even while her heart cried.

"Alyssa. I'm looking for Alyssa."

"Your name?" she heard the man murmur from a distance like he turned his face away from the phone.

"You have the right phone, but she doesn't want to talk right now. It's... Whoa. It's one o'clock. I need to get to work. Gotta go, lady." The phone went dead.

Sucking in a breath, Kim allowed her hand to drop slowly to her lap, checking to make sure that the phone was off before she just sat there.

Lord? My daughter. I love her. Please take care of her. Bring her back to You.

Was there anything else she could do? Prayer didn't feel like much, but it was everything. God could do anything. Even bring her daughter back.

Whatsoever things are pure, whatsoever things are lovely, whatsoever things are of good report…think on these things.

Snippets of a verse she'd memorized years ago came back to her.

Maybe that was the Lord prompting her, she wasn't sure, but she almost laughed. What good could she see in this situation?

But at least whoever was with her daughter today had a job. Hopefully it wasn't a job dealing drugs, and despite the horror that that thought filled in her soul, she laughed. Well, there were always good sides and bad sides, she supposed.

Her daughter was alive. That was good. God was faithful in His promises, and He could do anything. That was something else that was good.

She started thinking about things she could be thankful for. Thankful for the health of the baby she carried, thankful that Davis was there to help her start her business. Thankful that they talked about horses at the diner and Griff had come and made his offer. There were a lot of things to be thankful for. She didn't have to always look at the negative and allow it to get her down.

With that thought, she smiled a little to herself, leaned her head back on the back of the couch, and slowly drifted off to sleep, dreaming of horses and business and daughters that came home, and lacing through it all were the deep blue eyes of a man who was steadfast and sure.

Chapter 11

"I don't want to fight with him. If that's what he wants, give it to him."

"Are you sure? He really doesn't deserve this much. You've already given him way more than he had any right to ask."

"I know. But I don't want to fight, not if we can help it, and if this can be settled amicably by me giving a little bit more than what I need to, then that's what we'll do." Davis held the phone to his ear while he laced his shoes. He was three miles down the beach, in the middle of his run, getting ready to turn around, when his lawyer had called. He was a little early for most law firms, but his lawyer was unusual in that he ran early hours so he could get off early and go boating.

That worked just fine for Davis, and they'd had a good working relationship for years. Although, Jerome had not been very happy with Davis's insistence that Todd get whatever he wanted as they dissolved their partnership.

There was no way Davis could continue to be a partner with Todd after what he'd done to Kim, even if Davis weren't thinking that hopefully Todd's former wife would decide to be his.

He smiled, thinking about their lunch yesterday, and the way her hair fell around her face, the way she was concerned about Charlotte and Griff and even about Davis. The struggle she had taking over her own house and putting Davis out.

He could see it was still an issue for her. And he loved that. Loved what it said about her, and how it showed that she cared.

He guessed that if she weren't pregnant, she would have insisted on taking the stable apartment herself.

He supposed they would have ended up fighting over who got to live in the stable.

"All right. I'll have some papers for you to sign when you make it back down this way. How soon do you think that's going to be?"

"I don't know. A week. Maybe two." He didn't want to think about work, think about leaving Strawberry Sands.

"Is that the best you can do for me? You're not sure? A week or two?"

"I know. You have a busy schedule, and you'd like to have me penciled in, but... I really don't know."

He wasn't going to schedule anything if he could be helping Kim. All the things that he thought were important in the first part of his life didn't seem important at all now. Especially now that he knew Kim was carrying his child.

That made him smile even bigger. While he knew having children wasn't all peaches and roses, he loved that there was a connection that kept Kim from totally walking away from him.

"If you wanted to do something nice for your wife, if you wanted her to know that you love her, what would you do?"

Davis almost kicked himself. Men didn't ask other men that question. Not unless they were in counseling.

His lawyer grunted. And then he said, "You know you're on the clock."

"I'll pay for this."

"I'm divorced."

"And what did you learn from that?"

"You're still on the clock."

"I'm still paying."

"I learned that women are liars and cheaters and they're after your bank account. And if they find one that's bigger than yours, they'll ditch you pretty fast for it."

"Ouch. What'd you learn about yourself?"

"I'm still on the clock."

"And I'm still paying. Charge me double if you want to, because I want your honest answer."

"All right. Double time. I learned I'm a jerk."

"And what are you doing about that?"

"Triple time?"

"Stop it. We both know you're not going to charge me extra. And you're not going to charge me for personal advice. What are you going to do about it?"

"I'm not sure I want to do anything. It's uncomfortable to change. And I'm not uncomfortable enough to want to. You know? You have to dislike where you're at enough to think that you need something new before you actually start to change. In my case, I have no interest in getting married again. An occasional hookup, a few dates with different women, and I go home to my condo every night, don't have to worry about some woman nagging me because she wants kids or because she wants me to work less, or because she wants me to watch less TV, get rid of my toys, or because she wants me to take a vacation, or wants to get a dog or wants to get rid of a dog. Or because I didn't take the trash out or water the plants or whatever. I can't say that I miss that, and I don't care if I ever had to put up with it again."

"Wow."

"Yeah. Go ask someone who has a successful marriage, not me. You couldn't have picked a worse person if you thought about it and tried."

That seemed sad to Davis. Maybe because he'd recently had an epiphany and was trying to turn his own life around. Part of what he was doing now with his lawyer.

He straightened, lifting his head and looking out at the orange glow of the morning sun on the water.

"You think you're going to be satisfied with that when you look back over your life?" He wanted to talk about death, but that wasn't what normal people did. Still, that was part of what had him changing course. Because he didn't want to look at a life that was wasted and wish he had a chance to do it over.

"Probably not. But I don't think about it. It would just be pointless."

Davis didn't think so, but he thanked Jerome and hung up, shoving his phone in his pocket and breaking into a jog. It seemed like if he were a true Christian, he'd be working on improving himself until the day he died. Because he loved Jesus, of course, but also because he wanted the woman he loved to be getting the very best man possible. Wasn't that part of wanting the best for someone?

Chapter 12

Kim picked up her cup of coffee and looked out the window. It was a beautiful morning and probably warm enough for her to go out without a sweatshirt.

Still, she grabbed her sweater from where she laid it over the kitchen stool, just in case it was chilly.

A knock at the door startled her, and she glanced up.

A woman she didn't recognize stood just outside the door, holding something in her hands.

Kim hurried to the door and opened it. "Good morning," she said, feeling far more cheerful than she'd felt for a very long time.

"Good morning. You must be Kim."

"I am," Kim answered, wondering how the woman knew her name.

"News travels fast in a small town. You ate at the diner yesterday. I run the day-care. You probably walked by it on your way there."

"I remember seeing it. Lots of little kids inside."

"Yeah. I have seven right now. And there will be more over the summer." The woman's eyes got big. "I'm Violet." She laughed a little and shrugged, since both of her hands were underneath the casserole dish she carried. "Sorry I can't shake your hand, but I wanted to bring you something."

"Oh, that's so sweet," Kim said, a feeling of warmth burgeoning in her chest from the thoughtfulness. "Come on in," she said, stepping back and waiting for Violet to enter so she could close the door behind her.

"Griff is always trying out new strawberry recipes. I think he thinks that because the town's name is Strawberry Sands, people are going to come here looking for strawberries. I don't know. Anyway, he asked if I could try his strawberry coffee cake he made a couple of days ago, and it was pretty good. So I asked him to make me a small one for you since I don't have time to bake anything with all the children I have at the daycare."

"Of course not. You're probably exhausted once they leave."

"I am. And I had to bring it out early this morning, before any of my kids arrive. I was afraid you wouldn't be up."

"Sometimes I'm not, but out here... It's... It's like you just feel compelled to get out of bed because it's so pretty outside."

Violet nodded her head like she knew exactly what Kim was talking about. "Isn't that weird? Although, in the winter when it gets dark and cold, I'm the opposite and I want to just snuggle down under the covers and not move for days on end. It's a good thing I have a job, or I would probably hibernate."

Kim laughed. "Kids have a way of getting you out of bed." She glanced at Violet's hand and noted the absence of a ring. She wanted to ask if any of the kids she watched were hers, but if they were, Violet probably wouldn't be here, since she didn't seem to have a husband at home to care for them. But in case Kim ever needed a daycare for her baby, Violet seemed like a great person to have.

"Are you accepting new children?" she asked with a hand on her stomach.

"I heard you were expecting. I didn't want to ask. That's a question that can go down all the wrong way if you ask it to the wrong person."

They shared some more laughter while Kim offered for Violet to take a seat. "Would you like a piece of cake? I heard through the grapevine it's really good."

"I'll sit down for a few minutes. But…" She glanced at her watch. "I need to leave by twenty till. My first kid gets there around seven, and sometimes his mom is early."

"All right. Sounds like you have enough time for a cup of coffee and a piece of cake and a little conversation."

"And yes. I'm definitely accepting new kids. Babies are especially fun."

Kim nodded as she grabbed the knife out of the drawer, holding it in her hand for a moment before she slid the door shut. She really didn't know much about babies. Other than what she knew from Alyssa being young. But that seemed like a lifetime ago. Would she remember what she needed to know?

Then she thought about labor and how painful that had been. She wasn't looking forward to doing that again.

She took a breath, pushing those thoughts aside, and turned back around.

"So tell me about town. I just moved in yesterday."

"But your mom has owned this cottage for years. I heard you were going to get horses and start renting them out again which will be really exciting. The Landry family has horse rentals on the beach, but those are for more serious riders."

"Yeah. We're hoping to get beginner horses. I rode some a long time ago, but I need to brush up on everything. We don't want to get started on horses we can't control or that will hurt someone."

"We?"

Kim closed her mouth. She hadn't realized she was saying "we," but she had been. She'd been thinking about Davis and herself as...not partners. Definitely not partners. She wasn't getting involved with any kind of partnership. That was too much like marriage, and she'd already been there, done that, and hated it.

But she had been thinking of him as...someone who was helping her. More than that. But there wasn't a name for it, not a name she was willing to use.

"Davis. He... He was renting this place from my mom, and I didn't know about it. It was the only place I had to stay, so he moved out to the stable."

She hated saying that. Stumbled over it. Didn't want to admit that she kicked someone out of the house he'd been living in. She wanted to clarify, say that he was rich enough to afford to live any-where he wanted to. That he had two other houses he could easily live in if he desired. But that really didn't make it any better. Just because a person had money didn't make it okay to be mean to them. Or to be inconsiderate in any way.

"I see," Violet said, holding her hands out to take the plate that Kim held out to her. "Thank you," she said. "I feel bad that you're serving me. I can get my own coffee."

"It's all right. It's already brewed, and all I have to do is pour it." Kim went to do that, and soon they were sitting at the small bar in the kitchen, pieces of delicious strawberry coffee cake in front of them along with steaming cups of coffee.

"This is really good," Kim said as soon as she swallowed the first bite.

"I don't know where Charlotte found Griff, but he was a godsend. They're talking about opening a bakery along with the diner, but business just hasn't been that good for them."

"Griff is the big guy with all the tattoos and earrings?" The one who told her about the horses. She was pretty sure that was him, but he was so tough-looking, it seemed impossible that he'd made the delicious strawberry coffee cake in front of them.

"That's right. He looks pretty tough, but he's a real sweetheart, and everyone in town knows that he's head over heels for Charlotte who doesn't seem to notice that he's alive. She has a crush on some fancy-schmancy lawyer that comes to town once in a while."

Kim nodded, taking that in. She'd noticed yesterday that Griff looked at Charlotte with adoring eyes, but she hadn't seen them together long enough to realize that Charlotte didn't return the sentiment.

"Are you sure they're not related somehow? Griff just doesn't seem like a short-order cook kinda guy, let alone a great baker."

"I know, right?" Violet said, lifting her eyebrows and looking over the forkful of coffee cake that she held in the air. "I think everyone was shocked when he got off his bike, hung his helmet up, and decided to stay. Charlotte most of all, but I feel like it was love at first sight for Griff." Violet sounded a little bit dreamy and romantic. Which made Kim wonder about Violet's own past.

"You're not married?" she asked, with what she thought sounded like casual interest. She appreciated Violet coming, bringing the coffee cake, making her feel welcome, and giving her some details on the various people in town. It made her feel like a part of the community. Small towns cared about each other, and part of caring about someone was knowing what they were doing. She supposed it was termed small-town "gossip," but she didn't think about it as malicious, evil, sinful gossip. It was the kind of gossip that helped people know about each other, not the kind of gossip that spread ugly rumors and nasty stories about other people.

"No. But I've always loved kids. I taught school in inner-city Detroit for a while. And Lake Erie is pretty, but there's just something wild about Lake Michigan that I love. Plus, I grew up in Strawberry Sands, so it was natural to come back here. I took a bit of a pay cut. To say the least."

"Sometimes we have to in order to make our lives work. Money isn't everything." Kim meant that. But it was nice to have money in order to pay one's bills. She worried about that a little bit. She wasn't used to being the sole breadwinner, the only person providing for another human being.

Having to take care of herself was a completely different story than to have to take care of herself and another life. Todd hadn't been much of a husband, but he at least had been someone that she'd been able to say was beside her, and he gave the illusion of support; even if he wasn't around much, he helped pay the bills, anyway.

"So is that little church on the hill an actual church? Or is it closed?" Kim asked, changing the subject and pushing the thoughts of Todd aside. She had to get over it. He was a part of her life, but that part was in the past. And yes, she thought she was going to have a lifetime relationship with him, and she still wasn't quite over the pain of losing those girlhood dreams, the idea that she would grow old with the same person that she'd been young with once, but she was working on it. And eventually, whatever her life became was what she would accept and just pray that God could use her where she was. Whatever that looked like.

"It is! And we would love to have you. Pretty much everyone in town goes. Our pastor is really good, and he does preach from the Bible, but it's also a great time to get together. You'll meet almost all of your neighbors there."

"So it's like the community building?" Kim asked, having noticed that Strawberry Sands was too small to have one.

"Exactly. The community building, any kind of town clubs, or anything like that.

It all happens at church. Which is kind of funny," she laughed a little, "since the church is so small. Although there is a basement, thankfully, or we wouldn't be able to eat together in the winter. It's way too cold outside, as you probably know. You grew up in Blueberry Beach with Iva May, right?"

Kim nodded, loving that Violet knew her history. "I think I'm a little bit older than you, but we were practically neighbors growing up."

"My school was much smaller than yours. My elementary school anyway. They've combined all the high schools into one big building and ship the kids in to a central location. I don't really like that, but I guess it's more cost-effective or something." She shrugged, and Kim got the idea that it really didn't matter since she didn't have children.

It was something Kim was going to have to think about.

"So do you have any business advice for me?" she asked, glancing at her watch and realizing that Violet was going to have to leave soon. "I'm nervous. I've never owned my own business. And the idea that there will be horses to take care of and expenses and feed and I'll have to depend on being able to generate income... It's scary."

"I don't think you can think about all of that. You're going to try your best." Violet shrugged her shoulders. "Maybe you'll make it, maybe you won't. But you'll do your best. And I can guarantee you that the town will be behind you. They'll support you whatever you do. So you know that there is that."

"That's a nice thought. But I want to make it work myself. I guess, it does take a little pressure off when you think that all you can do is do your best. Still, it's scary."

"So you just hold tight to God's hand and take the jump. That's what I did when I opened up the daycare. I didn't have any kids signed up when I opened the doors. In fact, I think it was two weeks before I got my first kid. I did a lot of praying those two weeks. That's one thing about owning a business, you have a tendency to get closer to God." Violet paused. "Or become an alcoholic. One of the two."

"I can't have alcohol right now, so I guess that limits my options. It was the one I would have chosen anyway," Kim said as Violet grinned and nodded.

"Me too. That's just life, you know? Things work out, things don't. It's really not about us. We think it is, and we hear it is all the time, but it's not about our success necessarily, it's about living for the Lord. We get so confused, and that's where a lot of our stress comes from. We put it on ourselves, but God doesn't demand that we're successful in the world's eyes, He doesn't even demand that we're monetarily successful. He does tell us that we have to work, because the Bible says that a man who won't provide for his family is worse than an infidel, but he doesn't say that our businesses or anything that we try always has to work out."

"No, I guess it's just the concern about what other people are going to think about you."

"Exactly. And that's not supposed to bother us at all. Although it does. It's all about the show and the way things look, and we forget to be concerned about the deeper things of the heart. And we're even less concerned about just allowing God to guide us, even if that involves failure. We act like failure is this truly terrible thing, but sometimes we have to fail in order to succeed, in order for God to grow us, use us, humble us, and increase our character however He wants."

Kim nodded, thinking hard. She supposed the "failure" of her marriage was a great case in point. She hated that it hadn't worked out. It made her sad even now thinking about it. Even though she didn't really want to be with her husband, it was hard to think that she put so much effort into her marriage and still had failed.

But she knew that Violet was right. God could use her where she was despite what looked like a failure standing in front of her.

"Oh my goodness. The time flew by so quickly. Thanks so much for inviting me in, and it was really great to talk to you, but I need to run." Violet stood up, and Kim stood more slowly after her.

"I appreciate the coffee cake. If you see Griff, tell him it was delicious."

"I'll do that. Sometimes they bring me leftovers from the diner for the kids in the evening. And once all the kids are gone, sometimes I go in for a quick supper, if I'm too tired to cook."

"Yeah, I know all about that, and I only had one."

Kim walked slowly with Violet to the front door while Violet chattered about the town and how welcoming people were and Kim's pregnancy and asked her about due dates.

By the time Violet left, Kim felt like they were on the way to becoming really good friends. Which, she had to admit, made her happy, since it made her feel less alone.

Checking her watch, she had more than three hours until she was scheduled to meet with Davis to tour the stable and the old barn that sat back on the hill. She wasn't even sure whether that was in any shape to be used, although if it was, it would be a great place to store hay.

Regardless, she turned back to the bar where she'd left her coffee, when she heard gravel crunching and looked out the window. Her heart dropped. It was Todd.

Chapter 13

Was it terrible that upon seeing her ex-husband, Kim's first impulse was to hide?

Impossible to do with all the windows in the cottage, but even if it were possible, she hoped she would have resisted the urge. She needed to face her demons and fight her battles.

Lord, help. Please.

She didn't even know what she needed help with. Who knew what he wanted.

But the fact that he'd come the whole way to Strawberry Sands did not bode well.

Their divorce was final; he was already remarried and had a child.

He can't hurt you. He has no attachments to you whatsoever. Relax.

Just before he closed the door of his car, the thought ran through her mind that he might be there to see Davis. After all, they were partners. Or had been. Davis had said that he was cutting ties with her ex. Maybe she should have inquired a little bit more deeply. After all, did she really want to be doing business with Davis, or at least allowing him to help her, allowing him to live on her property, when he was still involved with her ex?

She really probably couldn't get him off of her property. He'd signed the lease. He said he had it. She didn't know exactly what those things entailed, but she already felt guilty that he moved out of the house. She certainly couldn't kick him off the property, so maybe she would have to put up with her ex.

But Todd turned toward the house.

Maybe he didn't realize that Davis had moved into the stable.

For some reason, Kim didn't want him to know either.

But she wasn't going to lie, although she wasn't going to volunteer the truth. Todd had no right to know anything about her.

She waited until he knocked before she moved the rest of the way to the door to answer. He was smirking, like he knew she'd been standing there like a deer caught in headlights.

"Todd," she greeted him, knowing that as a Christian she should summon up a "good morning," but just couldn't.

Todd, charming as always, and handsome as sin, with his dark eyes and wavy hair that parted on the side and brushed across his forehead, smiled his flirtatious smile at her. It disarmed her. Why was he being so nice?

"Good morning, Kim. What a beautiful morning, and you're looking fantastic as always."

It wasn't what he said to her when he left her. Something about her being dumpy and frumpy with a personality to match.

"Did you need something?" she asked, standing in the doorway and not inviting him in. She should. She should be kind and gracious, loving, the way God wanted her to be. Frustrated with herself, she backed away, forced a smile on her face, and said, "Would you like to come in?"

That sounded good. Kind, sweet. And like she was working through her anger and not catering to it on purpose.

"Why I'd love to. I actually want to stay in the area for a couple days and was hoping I could stay here with you."

"No!" That slipped out, louder and more forceful than she intended. She modulated her voice. "It certainly wouldn't look very good if you and I were living in the same house, would it?"

"It wouldn't be living with you. I would just be visiting. Staying for a few days. There's nothing wrong with that."

"It would make me uncomfortable. So, I'm sure there are some very nice houses and hotels and places to stay in Blueberry Beach. I could help you find one if you'd like."

He tilted his head as she closed the door. "Now, Kim, baby, you sound a little angry. There's no need to be angry. We can be adults about this."

Her teeth clamped down on her tongue. It probably affected the way her smile looked, but she wanted to be kind, despite how annoyed and angry she felt.

"Coffee?" she managed to say, loosing her tongue for that one word before clamping down on it again.

"Please. You always made the best coffee."

She wouldn't be taken in by his charm. She'd been young and stupid when he charmed her the first time. She'd been with him enough years to know that he was kind to people when he wanted something and then dumped them without a second look when he was finished with them. Todd was the most important thing in Todd's world.

"I have a pot that I made this morning. It's still warm." She indicated a chair and grabbed a cup out of the cupboard. It was the last clean one, since she didn't have a whole lot of extras. She wasn't even sure whether these were Davis's cups that he had left, or if they were mugs that her mom had dropped off at the cottage. She made a mental note to ask Davis about them. It had been kind of him to leave them if they'd been his.

"I'm not angry, but I know you're here because you want something. If you'd get to the point, I'd appreciate it. I have plans for later this morning, and I need to get some things ready." That was true. She wanted to get an idea of her vision for the riding business she was starting. She knew she was doing it haphazardly, but she didn't have much of a choice.

She needed something to do, needed to move forward quickly.

"We can at least exchange some pleasantries. We don't have to be uncivilized."

"We've exchanged pleasantries. I'm getting you coffee. Please tell me what you want."

She said a quick prayer of thanks to the Lord for somehow enabling her to modulate the anger she still had toward her husband and for being able to speak in a fairly rational tone.

She also hadn't hit him with anything, yet, and she sent up another small prayer of thanks for the self-restraint. Or maybe she should thank the Lord for hiding the skillet.

Whatever.

"I thought you talked about getting back together. I turned over a new leaf, I thought about some of the things you said to me and realize that I have a lot of room to improve, and I've been working on—"

"Your girlfriend left you already?" she interrupted him, because she couldn't help it.

"I married her. She was my wife. And she didn't leave me. We decided to mutually part. Amicably. We're sharing custody of the child, of course."

Kim couldn't understand why in the world it would benefit him to come back to her, but she had zero interest. Now, if she could just be kind about the way she said it. Even though she wanted to turn him down flat and send him on his way, hoping to never see him again. After all, he was the one who cheated, and he was the one who wanted the divorce. She was the one who had to reconcile herself to those things. Now that she started healing and moving on, she wasn't going back. No way.

"I'm sorry. Maybe before the divorce was final... Actually, I'm sure of it. I would have been willing to work on things up until we signed the papers. Once we did that, it was final, and there was no point in going back. That's how I feel about it."

"Now, Kim. We have history. We've been together since you were in college. That's a long time for two people to spend together. Surely all of those memories mean something to you?"

"Of course they do. You were a part of my life for decades. More than half of it." She couldn't just turn off her life. Forget the things he had done. Even though he hadn't spent a whole lot of time with her, his presence was everywhere.

"That's my girl. Remember how we used to look at the tall penthouse buildings and say how that would be us one day?"

They'd had a dumpy apartment in a not very good part of Chicago for a long time. And she laughed. It was like she was back to where she started. Only she wasn't looking for a penthouse anymore. She'd been there, done that, and didn't want to do it again.

"I remember. Those are good memories." That was back before he decided that work and other women were more important than her.

"You were pregnant with Alyssa. We'd sit there on the back porch, feeling the baby move and dreaming. Those were beautiful days," he said.

She nodded in agreement.

"We could have all of that back. I've grown and changed, and you have too. We know each other. We used to like each other. I'm sure we could again."

"I'm sure we could," Kim said, not wanting to disagree with him, because he was probably right. Still, she was firm in her conviction. She had no desire to go back down that road.

She was opening her mouth to say so when a voice came from behind her.

"Todd. I didn't know you were here."

Kim turned, trying to control her surprise. How had Davis gotten in? He hadn't come in the front door.

Still, she wouldn't confront him about that, not while Todd was there. She wasn't interested in a relationship with anyone, but her loyalty no longer lay with Todd. Between the two men, she was definitely with Davis. He had been the one who had treated her well. So far anyway.

"Good morning," she said with a genuine smile and took a couple of steps toward him.

She wasn't quite sure how it happened, but his arms spread out, and somehow she ended up giving him a hug. Her belly between them made it slightly awkward, and she turned to the side so she could fit a little better, a natural thing she didn't think about, as his arms squeezed her tight, and she felt him drop a kiss on her temple.

"Good morning. You're looking beautiful as always."

That was so odd. She looked up into his face, a little confused.

He looked down at her with a comfortable smile, a little bit of adoration in it, if she had to guess. Was that for Todd's sake? Or maybe hers. Maybe he'd heard what Todd was saying and was offering her his help.

"I can't believe you're living with someone," Todd said, a little bit of the derision that she was more familiar with than his charm creeping back into his voice. "You weren't even going to let me stay here for a day or two." He paused. "But that shouldn't matter if you're already living with someone. Were you just being mean?"

"Maybe she's just trying to protect herself from any more bad memories." Davis's words were easy, even though there was a hard edge to them. She turned slightly, and he kept his arm around her shoulders, keeping her close.

Maybe it was a show of possessiveness, which she wasn't sure whether she liked or not, but she allowed it to slide. She actually would prefer to let Todd know that she was not available.

"I thought you said that it was just a one-night stand with her?" Todd asked, looking at the arm around her shoulders and then back to the man who stood beside her.

"I don't recall talking to you about it at all." Davis's words were not friendly.

"All right. I made some assumptions. After all, I didn't see you with her after that night at all, ever."

"I guess you and I weren't together all the time, were we?" Davis asked. "Speaking of, I spoke with my lawyer this morning. He'll have some papers for you to sign. I'm just going to give you all the things you asked for, and that should be all we need to do to separate the partnership."

"Really?" Todd's brows went way up at that admission, and Kim wondered what in the world Todd had demanded that Davis give.

And why had Davis capitulated? Was he going to have anything left after he separated from her ex? She certainly hadn't.

She felt a little bad and wanted to interject herself into the conversation, wanted to fight on Davis's behalf. To make sure that he would have something to show for the years they'd been in business together. But she kept her mouth closed. She didn't know anything about it, and she didn't want to push in where she wasn't welcome. Even if she was trying to help.

Todd's mouth pressed together, and he seemed to be thinking as he looked at the two of them. "Did you guys get married? Why didn't you tell me?" His brows lowered, and he looked at Kim like she kept her marriage a secret

"Every child should have a mother and father," Davis said, and Kim noted that he very clearly did not answer Todd's question. Either affirmative, which would have been lying, or negative. It made her think that he didn't want Todd to know they weren't married. Odd.

Maybe she'd been through too much, but that made her suspicious. Was there a reason Davis didn't want her to get back with Todd? Was there something that she had that Todd wanted, that Davis wanted too?

She racked her brain, trying to think what that could be, but couldn't think of anything. This cottage was all that was left. The stable and the barn and a few acres. She hadn't had it assessed, but Strawberry Sands was not exactly a major tourist attraction area, although the way Blueberry Beach was growing... Maybe the ground was worth more than what she thought.

She hated the idea that Davis was only into her for what she owned. She could hardly believe it, because, after all, the one night they'd spent together, he hadn't known anything of the sort.

Todd, on the other hand, had a long history of being nice to people who could get him what he wanted.

"I'm not sure I understand why you're here sweet-talking Kim. Where's your wife?"

Todd's face hardened before he said, "We've mutually agreed to separate." It was like he deliberately relaxed his face as he smiled at Kim. "After all, it's hard to find anyone who compares to Kim and what we had together. I was hoping we could work on getting that back. I was actually here discussing that with my wife when you showed up. I take it you're not married?"

Davis had neatly sidestepped the question to begin with, but she should have known that Todd wouldn't be so easily brushed aside. Just the fact that he wanted to know if she was married, was almost demanding an answer, made her suspicious. This time, she answered.

"You heard him. The child should have a mother and father. That's our plan. And we are working together to open up the riding stable again. I think it's wonderful when married couples work together rather than separately. So many bad things can happen when you don't spend time with your spouse."

Todd's lips pursed as her words hit home. That's exactly what happened to them. He'd been far more interested in what was going on at work, or maybe who he was hanging out with after work, rather than being interested in what he had at home. Who he had at home.

"I'll take a look at those papers once my lawyer gives them to me," Todd said, walking over to where they stood. They shifted just slightly so he could go out the doorway, and Davis's arm stayed around her shoulders as they followed him to the front door.

"Have a safe trip home," Davis said as Todd opened the door.

"I'm sure I will," Todd said before he nodded his head and walked out.

Kim couldn't hold back her sigh of relief. She hadn't realized how much tension she'd been holding in her body while he had been in her house.

"Thank you for coming. How did you get in?" she said, turning to Davis and not saying the things she wanted to, like thank you for saving me. Thank you for being here. Thank you for your support. I don't want you to move because it feels so good to be held by you.

Chapter 14

"I came in the back door," Davis said, his arm still around Kim. He didn't want to let it go, liked the way she felt against him too much. Even though there was a riot in his chest that he hadn't quite gotten subdued because of the small bit of conversation he'd over-heard between Kim and Todd.

He'd seen Todd work women before. He was very charming, very sweet, very flat-tering, which definitely worked to get women interested and warmed up to him. Unfortunately, he never followed that flattery up with any kind of substance. And he ditched them as soon as he got what he wanted. Usually after one night, although it was Kim, and Davis wasn't sure exactly what Todd wanted with her.

"I saw the back door, but I didn't realize it wasn't locked."

"It was. I forgot to give you the key, and when I saw Todd's car pull in and realized he was here to talk to you and not me, I grabbed it and walked over. I... I wasn't sure how you two left things between you, and I didn't want you to end up here by yourself. I hope you don't mind I...acted like there was a little bit more between us than what there really was."

He wasn't sure whether he should apologize for that last part. He didn't want her to get the idea that he didn't want there to be anything between them. He did. He just didn't want to put her in a situation where she was uncomfortable.

"I appreciated it. I'm not sure what Todd wanted, but it made me wonder if the cottage might be worth more than what I thought it was. He seemed rather pushy, and I'm not so stupid as to believe it's because he actually wants me back."

She sounded sad. Like she accepted the fact that a man couldn't want her for her, he'd just wanted her for her money or whatever she could provide for him.

That made Davis angry, but he tried to tamp down the feeling. Because it also made him want to hold her and tell her that not all men were like Todd, and that she was beautiful and precious and amazing and there was so much about her that he couldn't even think of where to start.

Her character, her desire to do right, her willingness to admit when she was wrong and to want to do better.

As much as he loved the night that they spent together, he loved even more that she felt as guilty about it as he did.

That she was keeping the baby. That she told him about it immediately. She had had to. He might still not know that she was pregnant if she hadn't said anything.

"I'm not entirely sure he doesn't want you back, but I am entirely sure that you would be wise to resist. I can have my people look into how much this property is worth, if that would ease your mind."

"You don't know?" Kim looked at him with questions in her eyes, but he couldn't read any accusation there. The idea that she might think that he was after her for her money, or property, somehow infiltrated his brain from whatever the look was on her face.

He gritted his jaw, annoyed that she would lump him in with someone like Todd.

"I don't know. I rented from your mom because of the connection to you, but not because of any idea that the property might be worth anything. However, because of my business connections, and the different things I've been involved in, it would not surprise me at all if property values in this area have skyrocketed because of the growth of Blueberry Beach. It's working its way north, and it stands to reason that there is potential for development along the shore. That's all I can say right now, but it won't be hard to figure out."

"You've already offered to do so much for me, I hate to take you up on anything else."

"Then think about it like I'm satisfying my own curiosity."

She nodded and turned away a little. He loosened his hold. He didn't want to keep her when she wanted to leave, but he did wish that he could push past her resistance. Although, that resistance probably came more because of the pain she suffered at the hands of Todd than from any resistance to him. At least, that was going to be his working assumption.

And he knew, because of that, it was just going to take time for her to see he wasn't just a charmer, with no substance behind all the flashy, pretty words he threw at her. That he wasn't going to use her and then ditch her when someone else better came along.

He wished that was an easy thing to show, but he figured he just needed to settle in for the long haul.

Realizing that she might not choose him even after all of his effort.

It would be so much easier if he could be guaranteed the ending, but that wasn't something that happened for anyone.

"It looks like you had a busy morning. I can leave so that you can take a break before we meet again." He hoped that was being considerate. He didn't really want to go, but he heard that pregnant women were often tired. And her face did seem a little drawn, her shoulders a little droopy.

She finished pulling away from him and nodded. "If you don't mind, I think I'm going to sit down and put my feet up. It does feel like it's been a busy morning, and I know that the rest of the day is going to be full. Although," she said, almost as though she'd forgotten. "The daycare owner, Violet, brought me a strawberry coffee cake that Griff made. Would you like a piece before you leave?"

He'd never heard of strawberry coffee cake, but if it meant spending a few more minutes with Kim, he'd eat frog legs.

"It's so hard for me to picture Griff with an apron on stirring batter to put in the pan and bake in the oven," Kim said as she moved into the kitchen, graceful despite the swelling of her stomach.

He enjoyed just watching her. The simple sway of her hips, the easy and unaffected movement of her limbs. The swish of her hair down her back, and the calm huskiness of her voice as she spoke.

Her scent lingered in the air, soft and gentle and refreshing. It was unique, and mixed with the strawberry scent that drifted up from the coffee cake, it felt perfect. He could wake up to this every morning.

But she had been talking about Griff. "I think there's probably more to Griff than meets the eye. Although, I think he's working at the diner because of Charlotte."

"That's what I thought too, and Violet said that when she came. That must be one of those things that everybody knows but Charlotte."

"She did seem oblivious, although I think she's probably not the only woman in that position."

He didn't mean that as a slam or anything, just thinking that Kim didn't seem to understand how deep his feelings for her went. It seemed she still saw him as a one-night stand, although he admitted to renting the cottage from her mother because he knew of the connection to her.

She hadn't had any comment about that.

Patience. Have patience.

She pulled two plates from the cupboard and set a large piece of cake on his and served herself a much smaller one.

"I already had one. I'd like to say that I hate for you to eat alone, but it was just really good, and I'm going to have another while you eat."

"You're feeding two."

"But the second one is much smaller, and this is most likely going straight to my hips."

"I guess I'm not worried about it, other than seeing you be healthy," he said, wanting to tell her that her hips were perfectly fine, better than perfectly fine, but he figured that would make her uncomfortable at this point in their relationship.

"Have you ever been to the little church on the hill?" she asked as she settled in her seat.

"I go pretty much every Sunday. It's a great place. From what I understand, it's where everyone goes Sunday morning, so if you want to meet the folks of the community, that's the place to be."

"That's what Violet said this morning. I figured I would go, and it's always nicer if you know someone."

"You want to go with me?" He probably shouldn't have asked, because he didn't think that she was saying it as a hint, but he couldn't pass up the opportunity. What was the worst that could happen? She'd tell him no, and he'd be disappointed but not deterred.

"I'd love to," she said, and the pink that stained her cheeks made her look adorable and cute. He wasn't quite sure where it came from.

She wasn't stiff-arming him, pushing him away, so it encouraged him to push a little.

"I usually walk. Is that okay?"

"Absolutely. Even if it's raining, I think I have an umbrella around here some-where."

"There's one in the closet. I've used it a time or two."

"All right. Oh! I meant to ask you if the dishes here are yours."

"Some of them. Some of them were here. I wasn't going to try to differentiate between the two. It's not that big of a deal."

She nodded, and a small cloud passed over her face, like him mentioning that buying a few dishes wasn't exactly a hardship for him made her sad somehow.

"Money isn't completely evil." He wasn't sure if that was the issue or not, but he threw that out there.

"I know. I guess..." She sighed. "I just wish life were simple, you know? That people said what they meant, instead of trying to flatter you and take advantage of you when you're not suspecting it. That you just knew whether people liked you or not, and they didn't pretend to if they didn't, or... I don't know."

"I think I get it. But it's wishful thinking, because life is never going to be simple.

Even the idea of simple times is really an illusion. Because those sweet sunsets on the porch still come after a day of work, which is done because you have a mortgage on the place and you don't have a choice."

"I know. But they're pretty pictures to look at and to think about, aren't they?"

He nodded, liking that she understood what he was saying.

They chatted a bit more, with him expressing surprise at how good the strawberry coffee cake was and with silences that did not feel uncomfortable or awkward.

As they sat at the table with their empty plates in front of them, Kim said, "Did you have plans? Because, even though it's been a busy morning, I guess I'm kind of eager to get started on our business plan and trying to figure things out. I... I'm excited about it. Violet and I talked a little, and I admitted to her that I was scared, and she had some great words of encouragement for me."

"You don't need to be scared," he said right away, feeling bad that he hadn't been the one to reassure her, although he was glad that she had someone. And he was glad that she was admitting it now.

"I know. I just... I know you'll help me however you can, but that in itself makes me nervous, you know?"

"How?" he asked, suspecting he already knew the answer.

"We already talked about how a partner-ship is a lot like a marriage. I guess... I guess I've just been burned before, and I feel like the only person I can depend on is myself, and the idea that I'm de-pending on you makes me feel not just like I can't do it on my own, but also like I don't want to be constantly wondering whether or not the person who's doing business with me, like the person who was doing life with me, is going to quit on me."

"Would it make you feel better if we sign a contract between us?" He couldn't think of how else to ease her mind.

"There was a contract between Todd and me. He broke it."

"Right."

"I'm sorry. It must be really insulting to you to think that I'm comparing you to Todd. I'm really not."

"Thanks. Because yeah. I appreciate the fact that you acknowledge that there's a difference between the two of us."

"For sure. I just know I need to proceed with caution. I feel like the divorce really messed Alyssa up. I don't want to do that to this baby."

"Of course not. I appreciate the fact that your baby is an important part of your consideration."

"She is for sure. Actually, I wondered if I'll even be able to do a boarding stable with a newborn. How am I going to go out and muck stalls this winter?"

"That's a good question." He'd be willing to muck stalls, but she had just said that she didn't want to depend on him, so that offer wasn't what she needed. Not until she could believe that he would stay. But he couldn't force that belief for her.

"You know, sometimes you just have to trust. Sometimes that trust is broken, and sometimes you just have to go on."

"I know."

"Anyone who has a business can't depend on their employees to stay. Sometimes better opportunities come up, and you just have to let them go. It's... It's hard, and you appreciate people who are loyal, but you can't expect people to be loyal. Because, most of the time they're just not."

"And you can't blame them for wanting the best for their families."

"Of course not. New opportunities come up, opportunities that are better for their relationships or better for them. Although, it's always a little bit annoying when it's just a matter of money."

"Even still, you can't blame someone for wanting to go to a different job that pays better. We certainly would if it were us."

"You're right." He scraped the crumbs on his plate before he looked at hers and said, "Are you done? I'll take your plate."

She smiled, like him taking her plate was some kind of big deal. Of course, after he thought that, he tried to imagine Todd standing up and taking his plate to the kitchen, and it was a little bit difficult. Maybe she wasn't used to being with someone who wasn't afraid to pitch in and help with the housework.

In fact, he could totally see Todd thinking he didn't need to do anything around the house, that it was Kim's job.

How sad to be married to someone who only saw her worth as whatever he could get out of her.

She was so much more than that. He wondered if she'd ever see it.

Chapter 15

Late that night, Davis was in the stable, doing some of the carpentry work he and Kim had talked about.

He was satisfied, more than satisfied, with what they discussed earlier that day. They talked about a business plan, and they'd written down some bare-bones structure that should give Kim an idea of where she needed to go.

He didn't mention it to Kim, but he had made a mental note to talk to his lawyer to see if he could make sure that she and the baby were taken care of for the rest of their lives if anything should happen to him.

He had enjoyed their time together while she was making her plan, but he could see from the restless way she twisted her hands together, and how her foot was hardly ever still as they sat at the table, that she was nervous.

It was a big step to start one's own business and a lot safer to work for someone else.

At least it felt that way.

He almost wanted to counsel her to do it. He didn't want her to worry or to stress. And while his lawyer had not come back with a set figure, he'd also found out late that evening after Kim had left that her property was indeed worth millions.

She could sell it and be set for life. Apparently there were some regulations going into place further south on the beach, which made the unrestricted land by Strawberry Sands much more appealing to investors, hence increasing its value.

He wasn't going to keep that information from her, he just wasn't going to text it to her.

They'd talk about it on the way to church in the morning perhaps.

In the meantime, he'd been too restless to settle down to sleep, so he'd gone down to the stable and worked on replacing some of the loose boards and constructing a new birthing stall.

There was plenty of room that hadn't been used, and they had checked out the barn that sat a little ways away and decided it would be perfectly fine for hay storage, especially since it was one quarter full of hay.

Because of that, they decided a birthing stall would be a good addition.

He'd downloaded some books onto his reading app and figured he'd brush up on some of the things that he learned about horses when he was younger.

He'd been thinking about which book he wanted to start reading when a voice at the door startled him.

"Are you open for visitors?" the voice said.

Davis looked up to see a man who seemed to be about his age, perhaps slightly less tall, but with wide shoulders and a narrow waist, although his eyes were gentle and kind.

"Pastor?" Davis said, squinting. He hadn't seen Pastor out of church much at all, and the man looked different when he was wearing jeans and boots and a hat.

"You recognized me through my disguise," Pastor said.

Davis laughed. "Are you sure you don't wear your disguise on Sundays?"

"I guess it could be that. But I suppose both of them are the real me. I know it's kind of odd to think of a pastor as a real person. At least I had trouble with that before I became one myself."

"Yeah. I suppose. I guess we have a tendency to think that the pastor has all the answers and has his life together. That he doesn't need to work or just floats around eating manna all day or something." Davis snapped the measuring tape back on his waist and shoved his pencil back behind his ear.

Pastor laughed and nodded. "That's about what I get." He nodded at the board Davis held. "I used to work for a construction company. I can give you a hand if you want me to."

"Really? It'd sure be easier to put these boards up if I had someone to hold the other end."

"Not a problem. I can hold boards."

Davis figured that was an understatement, because if Pastor worked for a construction company, he could probably do a whole lot more than that.

"I heard the daughter of the woman who owns this house is here."

That probably wasn't all Pastor had heard, but he waited until he had used his skill saw on the board where he'd marked before he answered him.

"You heard correctly. I suppose you heard that she's pregnant with my child?" He figured he might as well face the issue head-on. That would be the thing he would least want to tell the pastor, so it probably ought to be the thing he first told him.

"Actually, no, I hadn't heard that."

"And I'm not married to her." He added that just for good measure.

"You don't have to confess anything to me," Pastor said, grabbing the other end of the board and following Davis as he walked to the stall to put it on top of the first five boards that had already started to form the wall for the stall that he was building.

"I just wanted to be sure that we started out straight. I didn't want to feel like I had to hide anything, and sometimes in conversation, it's harder to correct misconceptions and admit the truth, if someone makes the wrong assumption."

"It makes things less awkward to start with the hard stuff. I understand what you're saying. Still, your personal life is between you and the Lord. I'm not here to judge you."

"Of course not. But you are here to tell me if I'm heading down the wrong path, because God doesn't wink at sin, and I know you don't either."

"So you've been listening to the sermons I've been preaching. Seems like half the time I look out, it seems like everyone is staring off into space somewhere."

"I do listen. They've made a difference in my life for sure. I mean, I'd already decided to turn it around when I came here, but listening to you, knowing everything you say comes straight from the Bible, has been a huge part of me getting things in my life right. I still have a ways to go."

"Interesting. And how does the mother of your child fit into that?" Pastor asked, and the question didn't feel probing. It felt like the pastor was asking out of care and concern.

"I'd like to marry her. She fits in like that. I moved out of the house, because she didn't realize her mom rented it out. She recently passed away."

"Thanks for letting me know. Maybe I'll pay her a visit."

"I think she'd appreciate that. I think she's here for the long haul. Anyway,

I moved into the apartment above the stable here, so there's that."

"I wondered why you didn't confess you were living with her."

Davis held the drill against the screw and looked over at Pastor. His eyes held a twinkle. He was teasing.

"That's funny," Davis said, grunting, before he put the bit in the head of the screw and pulled the trigger, holding the board with his knee, grateful that the pastor had a hold of the other end. It did make it a lot easier.

"You said you wanted to marry her, but you didn't mention her wanting to marry you. I assume that's the hangup?"

"She had a bad divorce, a messy breakup. She's got a lot of hurt, and that's probably all I ought to say about that. Maybe she'll talk to you about it."

"I doubt it. I probably won't probe for any of her dirty secrets. I'll just welcome her and invite her to church."

"Well, a welcome is good, and you can invite her if you want to, but she's going with me."

"And that's fine," Pastor said, as though he caught a whiff of the idea that Davis was staking his claim. He supposed he was in a way, although that felt a little old-fashioned. Still, Kim was an appealing woman, sweet and funny and kind, and come to think of it, she'd make a perfect pastor's wife, although he guessed she had no interest in it. But yeah, he just wanted Pastor to know which way the wind was blowing.

"I take it that she's the one opening a riding stable?"

"She is. We are, I guess. I'm helping her."

"I see." The pastor stood back while Davis walked over to the other end of the board with the drill, screws in hand.

"I've been thinking about something, and it feels a little awkward to talk about," Davis began, then he put the screw on the board and screwed it in.

"All right. I guess I'm the king of awkward conversations, since I talk about death with a lot of people, and religion, which is not everyone's favorite subject. So go ahead, shoot."

Davis supposed that was probably true, Pastor was used to awkward conversations. Still, this was probably going to be more awkward than most, since he wanted to talk about emotions, and it certainly wasn't his favorite thing.

"I've been trying to think about things I can do to show Kim that I'm serious about her. She already told me she has trouble trusting. And I assume that is just going to take time, but still, I want to try to figure out if there is anything I can do."

"What are you doing now? Is she paying you for this?"

They walked back over to the pile of two-by-fours.

"No. She's not."

"Does she know you're doing it? Does she appreciate it?" Pastor indicated his watch. "It's probably not too many people that are going to be out at eleven o'clock, working on a business that is not theirs, for someone who's not part of their family."

That was a good point. If she were paying him, it wouldn't mean anything other than it was a job to him, but the fact that she wasn't... Maybe she could see that it was a labor of love. For her. He hadn't really thought of that.

"Kim isn't the kind of person who takes people for granted. But she might be a little suspicious of my motives. I just found out tonight the property is worth millions. Her ex was here today, which is what prompted me to check. She suspected he was being charming, and telling her he wanted to reconcile, because he wanted something. She was right."

"Ah," Pastor said, picking up the end of the board that Davis just sawed and carrying it over, placing it on top of the last one they had done. "I see. So doing this might just make her more suspicious."

"Exactly."

"I think you're right. It's going to take time. Time to see that it doesn't matter what she has or doesn't have, that you are going to be faithful, that she is your priority over every other woman, regardless if you're 'official' or not, and sticking no matter what. If that's what you're doing?"

"Yeah." Making her feel like she was more special than anyone else. Well, she could easily see that he wasn't flirting or helping or even chatting with any other woman. "I mean, she's going to have my baby, and that is definitely something that would keep me here, regardless of anything else, but it's not about the money for sure; it's about Kim herself."

Pastor nodded, his look thoughtful. "I'm sorry, but I'm not sure you can rush any of that. The Bible says a brother offended is harder to win than a strong city. I definitely think Kim falls into the category of someone who's been offended, and she is going to be doubly cautious and very hard to 'win.'"

"That's kind of what I thought."

"But it doesn't hurt to work on it. There are always things that we can do to be better."

"Yeah. And sometimes things just take time. I get it."

They worked in silence for a while and then chatted about the church and the things that were going on there while they finished putting up the stall wall.

"All right. I think I'm going to call it quits for tonight," Pastor said as he stepped back and looked at their work.

"Not too shabby for midnight," he said as he surveyed the wall they just built.

"I like it. I appreciate you helping me. Went twice as fast."

"Good company always makes time fly." Pastor waved, then started for the door. "I'll pray about it. I wish I could do more, but that is probably the best thing to do anyway. We always feel like we need action, where sometimes we just need faith and trust."

"That's true. I want to do it, but sometimes I need to step back and allow God to do it."

"Exactly. But that doesn't mean we stop looking for opportunities where God has opened the door and expects us to lend a hand."

"I'll keep that in mind. I definitely have my eyes open, and I'm looking."

Pastor nodded, then he turned and disappeared into the darkness.

Davis put his tools away as he thought about his conversation with Pastor.

He closed the stable doors and stood at the end, looking out across Lake Michigan.

If God could create all of that, create the stars above, and worlds that humans hadn't even discovered, he was certainly more than capable of taking charge of Davis's life.

It was a reassuring thought and one that settled down easy in his soul. He wasn't good at patience; in fact, he was terrible at having patience. But maybe that was part of what God was trying to teach him. After all, he didn't want to walk through this world never learning anything, and trials and hardships were the best teachers.

With that thought, and after glancing at the cottage which was completely dark, he turned and headed toward the steps and his apartment.

Chapter 16

As Kim got ready for church the next morning, she had a small discussion with herself. She'd been struggling with the guilt of pushing Davis out of the home that he had paid to rent. That he had signed a contract for.

She'd also been dealing with guilt for not trusting him like she knew she should, especially since he had been working so hard for her. Helping her with her business plan, planning to go with her to pick out the horses, and she'd been listening the night before to the sawing and drilling in the stable.

It wasn't that she had been unkind to him. She hadn't. But she wasn't happy with how things were between them, how she was holding up her side of their friendship. It felt like he was doing so much more than she was, and she didn't like that feeling.

And yet, the idea of letting go, of daring to trust again, seemed so hard.

She was still thinking about it as she left the house, walking out onto the path and finding that he was waiting for her.

"Good morning," she said, smiling.

"Someone had a good night's sleep," he said, grinning back at her.

He seemed to be so even-tempered. Whatever happened, he rolled with it, and his calm assurance was a great foil for her tendency to worry.

It was a tendency she was working on, because she knew the Lord was in control, and there was no need for her to be concerned, but it was still hard to lift her fingers off of everything she wanted to hold onto. To let go of her expectations for how things should unfold and turn out.

"I did. Although I heard you working in the stable until almost midnight."

"Did I keep you up?" he asked immediately, concerned.

"No. I just felt guilty. I hope you know that I appreciate so much all that you're doing. From the business plan to whatever you were doing in the stable last night, to going with me this afternoon to look at the horses."

He smiled, like her telling him that she appreciated him meant something to him. "It's my pleasure. And I'm serious about that."

"Hopefully I can pay you back."

"I just enjoy being with you." He didn't stop to let that sink in, although she loved the way that sounded. She didn't want to compare everything that ever happened to her with her ex, but that was one of the things that had hurt, when she had realized that he really didn't care about being with her. Didn't care about spending any time with her, didn't want to be around her.

"I don't need you to pay me back. But I did get a call last night from one of my people, and after just a cursory inquiry into land values in this area, it seems that your property is worth millions. How many millions, I'm not entirely sure, but definitely in the tens of millions. With almost a half a mile of beachfront, that really makes it valuable."

"Wow."

"Yeah. I was working last night, but I thought that you might have changed your mind about what you want to do once you heard that. You could be a millionaire if you decided to sell and get out."

"What would you recommend?"

He seemed to have so much business sense, and it seemed to be almost a no-brainer that selling would be the smartest thing to do. Businesswise. Although, the cottage was her mother's, and she loved the quaint little town of Strawberry Sands. She really didn't want to sell.

"I think that's probably up to you. But that should ease your mind. If the riding stable doesn't work out, if you can't make a go of the business, there is that to fall back on. I don't think you'll have trouble finding a buyer, especially if you're willing to take a couple million less than the going price, and you can definitely start fresh somewhere else. It would be up to you."

"Yeah." She spoke softly, thinking. Trying to imagine all the repercussions of selling. She hadn't even considered, until she heard millions. Should the amount of money her land was worth really influence her into changing the direction she was going? Not if she thought she was going in the direction God wanted her to. And she had been sure about that.

Was this just a red herring?

"So your recommendation would be to try, see if we can make it, and sell if it doesn't work out?"

"You want my honest opinion?" he asked, looking over at her as the breeze from the lake blew her hair and she pushed it back. The wind whipped her dress around his legs and made her smile, because it was so fresh and clean and gave her energy clear down to her toenails. If they weren't headed to church, she would have taken her shoes off.

"Yes. I want your honest opinion."

"I think anytime you go into something thinking that if it doesn't work, you have a backup plan, it's a bad idea. If you're going to do something, especially if you're going to go into business, but anything, our relationship, a job, even buying horses, whatever, I think you want to go into it with your whole heart and soul, thinking that you're going to do everything you can to make it succeed. If you go in with a backup plan, with an in-case-we-fail plan, you might not be desperate enough to see the options that you need to see in order to make it work."

"That makes sense. But now that I know how much the ground is worth, it's going to be really hard not to think about it like that."

"I didn't want to not tell you. I didn't want you to think I was keeping anything from you. Plus, it wasn't that hard to figure out. You could do it yourself."

"But I didn't. And I appreciate the fact that you're being honest. That you're not trying to hide things from me. That means a lot."

Certainly, especially after the relationship that she'd been in before, which had been a lot of Todd hiding things from her and lying to her, she was almost sure that if Todd knew what the property was worth, he wouldn't have told her. In fact, when he visited yesterday, he might have known. He definitely hadn't mentioned it.

There she went comparing them again. It was kind of hard not to though, since she was trying to get over her inability to trust, and it was good to see that Davis was a completely different man than Todd. That made it easier to let go and to believe him. To believe that he wanted the best for her and for their child.

"I have a midwife appointment next Friday. I was thinking about that last night too, that I wanted to make sure that you knew that you're welcome to come. If you wanted to."

She tried not to care whether he wanted to come or not, but she actually really wanted him to want to. Wanted him to want to be a father, wanted him to want to be involved and to take interest in his child, even though she wasn't born yet.

"I... I don't know what to say. Other than thank you. Thank you so much. I... I absolutely will go to everything you let me go to. I want to. More than anything. Not just for her though." He slanted a glance over at her, and her heart skipped a beat.

She drew in a breath and looked out toward the lake. She couldn't deny his words sent a thrill through her, but she didn't trust thrills. Not anymore.

"This is where we turn to go to the church," he said, indicating a path through the dunes and stairs that led up a short hill.

"I bet the view from the church is gorgeous," she said as they started toward it.

"It is. It's a beautiful church, a great congregation, and you're right, the view is amazing."

She tried to imagine how it might look in the winter, with snow coming in off the lake, with the wind blowing and cold, but it was hard to think about that with the sun shining so brightly and the breeze friendly and almost warm as they walked side by side and into the parking lot of the church which was already starting to fill out.

Davis hadn't been kidding when he said the whole town was there. She saw everyone she knew from Strawberry Sands and a lot of people she didn't.

She was given a warm welcome, as people came and, after asking about her plan to start the stable up again, thanked her for coming to town and hoping to rejuvenate businesses.

The sermon was a good one, the music simple and beautiful, and Kim couldn't believe how much sweeter and more restful in her soul she felt as she closed her Bible and stood for the last hymn and the invitation.

They chatted with Griff about a few more things as they walked to the steps, including Griff's strawberry coffee cake, before he walked off and they made their way down through the parking lot and down the steps to the beach.

"I put some chicken in the crockpot this morning before I left. Do you want to have lunch?" Davis asked as they reached the bottom of the steps and walked on the path through the dunes.

He sounded a little like he wasn't sure whether she would be happy to be eating with him or not, and that made her feel bad. She didn't mean for him to get the idea that she didn't like him. She did.

Quite a lot. He'd been nothing but solicitous to her since she came.

"Do you want to bring it to my house?" she asked.

"That would be easy."

"All right. Then since you made it, let's eat at my house, and I'll do the dishes."

"We could do the dishes together, and then everything will be cleaned up by the time it's time to leave. Do you mind if I drive?"

"No. I appreciate it." She almost asked him to stop being so perfect, to give her a reason to back away, but that was not fair to him. So she closed her mouth and thanked the Lord for giving her such a wonderful person, a wonderful man, a wonderful father to her baby. Maybe, in time, he would be more.

Chapter 17

"So, those are the horses that I have for sale that are safe for beginners. Of course, you never know exactly what a horse is going to do, so you can't guarantee that they'll never do anything wrong, but I can personally vouch that I've had each of them at least six months, and they've been beginner safe."

George Reynolds, the owner of the horse stable who Griff had recommended to them, strode down past the stalls of the horses they'd already seen.

"What about that one?" Davis asked, indicating a stall that they hadn't been to yet, where a nose stuck out between the bars.

"That's one I just got in. I... I'm not sure there's anything I can do for her; she's pretty bad."

Davis noticed that Kim had a hand on her stomach, and she was walking slower than she had been before. Her shoulders drooped a little, and her eyes weren't quite as bright. They'd spent more than two hours getting each horse out of their stall, looking them over, and listening to everything that George said about them.

She had to be exhausted.

He wasn't going to say anything more about the horse in the far stall, but to his surprise, Kim spoke up.

"You don't think there's anything you can do for her?"

"No. She is pretty far gone. One of my people got her off of the truck where she was headed toward the kill pen yesterday, but I think I might send her along. I hate to, but she's in pretty bad shape."

"Bad shape? You mean she's lame?" Kim asked as they stopped at the stall. She peered in.

"No. I mean she's extremely skinny, like she's been starved, and while she's not mean, she's spooky. Like she's afraid anyone who comes near her is going to hurt her. I don't want anyone here to get hurt."

Davis didn't know what Kim was thinking, but he was thinking that if it was just a matter of her being thin and needing a little bit of extra food to gain weight, he was down for that. Even if she was spooky. That might be something they could work with, too.

"You're going to send her back?" Davis asked just to confirm.

"I know. It's harsh, but you can't save them all. This one's going to take a lot of time, effort, and money, and I'm never going to get that out of her. Plus, it's going to take a lot of work to get her to trust people again."

Davis couldn't help but compare the horse to the woman beside him. It might be silly, but it seemed like the horse having trust issues mirrored Kim's own problems.

He looked at Kim, who was looking at him with her brows raised in question. He didn't have to hear her say anything to know she wanted the horse.

"Can we take her?" Davis asked.

"I thought you guys were just starting out? You're not going to turn a profit if you're putting all of your money into a horse that you don't even know whether you're going to be able to ride. Not to mention, if the public gets a look at her, you're going to have people complaining. They won't understand that you got her in that condition and didn't make her that way yourself."

"We'll just have to be sure that anyone who's in the stable knows what's going on. Or we can talk to animal control ourselves so they know what we're doing."

"That might be the smartest thing to do." George sighed. "If you're interested, I won't charge you for her. We can get her out, and you can look at her. But I'm warning you, she's not real steady on her feet. In fact, I'm kinda surprised to see her up."

"Maybe she'd do better to be out on pasture?" Davis suggested, thinking that if she got down in the stall, it'd be a lot harder to get her up than if she were out.

"If I were keeping her, that's where she'd be."

George grabbed the lead that was hanging over the hook by the stall door and hooked it on the mare's halter. He wasn't joking about the fact that she wasn't steady on her feet. She swayed from side to side, and a couple of times, Davis feared she would go down.

She didn't, but her head hung low, her fur was matted, and every single rib stood out in stark definition, as did her backbone. Her head seemed too big for her neck, and her eyes were dull and droopy.

"She looks like a little Arabian," Kim murmured. Her eyes swept over the horse, and Davis could tell that seeing the condition of the horse hadn't changed her mind at all. If anything, it had firmed her resolve.

He didn't know how anyone could look at the horse and not feel compassion, because he felt the same way Kim did.

"We'll take her," Davis said and was rewarded with a happy smile from Kim. Although her eyes still looked worried.

"All right, but I'm going to warn you, she might not be any good for what you guys are going into business for."

"She might not be, but every business needs to have something that they're doing to make the world a better place. I think this mare has a lot of potential, and she just might be perfect for us."

George didn't look like he was the slightest bit in agreement with her, but he didn't say anything.

They made arrangements for George to bring the horses out on Wednesday, and Davis wrote out a check before they left.

He had barely gotten his car door shut when Kim said, "I thought I was paying for them."

"It was nice of you to wait to argue with me until we got in the car."

"You're changing the subject."

"Hmm. That wasn't a subject change. I was just complimenting you."

"I'm writing you a check out for that amount. This is my business."

She didn't sound argumentative or even upset, just exasperated. Like she wasn't angry, and she wasn't even trying to assert the fact that it was her business. Just that she didn't want him paying for what she should be paying for. Kind of like she'd moved the relationship from casual friends to good friends.

He'd never really thought about the difference, and it prompted him to say, "So we're friends now?"

Maybe his voice was a little lower, a little huskier, a little more intimate than what the conversation indicated, but it made him happy.

"Of course we're friends. I can't have you doing everything that you're doing for me and not consider you a friend. I also can't have you doing it all and paying for everything as well. You're helping me, not paying the bills for me."

"You can't imagine how happy that makes me," he said, ignoring everything else she said, except for the fact that they were good friends.

"And you are exasperating me," she said, lifting her brows, but she didn't look exasperated. She looked happy.

"I think that little Arabian has a lot of potential. Although I think George might be right. She might never be very good as a horse we can rent out to customers."

"I had a little Arabian just like that when I was younger. Her name was Honey, and she and I rode up and down Blueberry Beach for years. I loved her so much.

When I went off to college, it just made sense to sell her, since I wasn't going to be around to ride her."

"That's life. It goes on, and things and people come in and out of our lives."

She looked over at him as he pulled out on the road, accelerating up to road speed before she said, "And some people stay."

Her tone intrigued him, and he glanced at her, liking what he saw. He nodded solemnly. He was going to be one of the people who stayed in her life. Not just because they had a baby together.

She smiled at him, and he thought that maybe she was softening toward him, maybe they were moving toward something more permanent, when her feet scrunched up, like she was in pain.

"The baby?" he asked immediately as her hand went to her stomach, and after a brief moment of surprise, her face turned down.

"I think so. But it shouldn't be. It's way, way too early." She kind of ended on a groan, and then she said, "But this hurts."

"I'll drive straight to the emergency room." They weren't far from the Blueberry Beach Hospital. Only ten minutes.

"I think you'd better. I think I might be...bleeding. Or... My water just broke." Her face twisted, and even though she was hunched over a little and he could tell she was in pain, she whispered, "Sorry about your car."

"Good grief, woman. Don't worry about the car. It doesn't matter." He couldn't believe she was even thinking about it. "How far along are you? The baby will need a ventilator, at the very least, right?" He wasn't sure what a full-term baby was or how far along they were until they didn't need to be intubated anymore, all he knew was that this was way too early and she needed the care of medical professionals and she needed it now and he couldn't stop to have the baby in the car if it needed to go on life support immediately after birth.

Then the idea that they might not just lose the baby, that he could lose Kim too, made him push even harder on the gas pedal which was already on the floor.

"Twenty-eight weeks. So not far enough. I don't know what that means," she said, seeming to grunt out her words like it hurt to talk.

Just the idea of her in pain made him panic and intensified the fear of losing either her or the baby or both.

Lord. Get us to the hospital, please. Keep them both safe.

He wanted to pray that God would give him the pain and take it from Kim, but he knew that was impossible. Maybe not impossible for God, but not something that was going to happen.

This was something Kim was going to have to go through, but at least God had orchestrated it so that he was with her. It could have happened two weeks ago when he hadn't been around.

It could have happened while she was at the house by herself.

He took the time to thank the Lord for choosing the timing when he could be there. Even if he wasn't any help, at least he was driving her to the hospital, which was so much better than the thought of her groaning on the floor of her cottage with no one around.

"We're almost there... Are you doing okay?"

"Yeah," she said, although she sounded anything but okay.

It felt like forever until he was able to pull up to the emergency room. He parked right in front of the doors.

He was going to have to move his vehicle, someone was, but he didn't care about that right now. All he cared about was getting her into where she needed to go.

He ran around the car, opened her door, and ignored that she was trying to get out on her own.

Putting his arms under her, he carefully moved her so that he didn't hit her head as he was lifting her around the car.

"I think I can walk," she said, the words pinched out.

"And I know I can carry you. Let me, please," he said, having absolutely no intention of putting her down regardless of whether she said he could or not. It just sounded better for him to ask.

She didn't insist, and he pushed through the double doors, impatient for them to open, and then walked boldly up to the desk.

He'd only made it halfway there when the woman behind it stood, her hand at her chest. "What is it?" she asked, her words clipped and short.

Thankful for small-town hospitals that typically didn't have a wait in their emergency room, he prayed they also had skilled surgeons and doctors in the ER. "Premature labor."

"All right," she said, pushing a button underneath the counter that opened the doors to a hallway that led back to exam rooms. "Set her on the first bed in room A, and I'll have the doctor there immediately."

"All right. Hurry, please," he said, grateful his voice sounded calm, although the rest of his body was panicking.

Kim tensed and doubled around her stomach, her head pushing into his chest, as her knees tucked up.

"Just hold on, just a little bit longer."

"I think I need to push. In fact, never mind. I know it."

He was at the doorway, and he forgot all about his calm, rational voice as he called over his shoulder, "She says she needs to push."

"Got it." A woman materialized beside him, holding a gown as he walked through the door and she followed closely.

Things went by in a blur from there, with someone getting Kim into the gown as the hospital loudspeaker called for a labor and delivery team to assemble, and the doctor strode into the room as Kim lay down on the hard hospital bed.

The doctor looked at him. "You're the father?"

"Yes."

The doctor jerked his head up. He put a hand on Kim's shoulder, which made her open her eyes. "We have a team coming, and we're going to do our best to take care of you and your little one."

He said a few more things, explaining what he was doing as he started examining Kim.

They allowed Davis to stay with her until they wheeled her away. The nurse who had brought the gown, who he assumed was in the ER and not a part of the labor and delivery team that eventually showed up, explained that normally the husband was allowed in, but because it was an emergency, she would show him to a waiting room, where they would let him know the outcome.

It wasn't busy; he was the only one in it as he paced from one side to the other, unable to sit down and be still. He was able to pray just as easily while he was pacing as he could on his knees.

Then, he decided that maybe the suggested position of being on one's knees wasn't just to show respect and humility, but it was also to calm oneself and allow a person to remember that God was in control.

At that point, he knelt down by one of the chairs, his forehead on the seat, his eyes completely closed while he breathed short prayers. Let her be okay. Let the baby be okay. Give the doctors wisdom. Give them what they need. Watch over them. Keep her safe.

He said the same things over and over again, but at least when he was praying, he was doing something, which was better than doing nothing. But after a while, his position, or just the ability to talk to the Almighty, calmed his soul to the point where he could speak in rational sentences, but he never stopped praying.

He was still in the position when the door opened. He looked behind him to see a man in scrubs, a blue cap on his head and a mask over his face, walk in.

"You're with Kim?" the man asked.

"Yes," Davis said, getting to his feet and walking to the doctor.

He didn't want to attack the man, but he wanted information, and he wanted it right away.

"I'm Dr. Walters. Kim delivered a very small baby girl by C-section. The baby looks healthy, other than being just two pounds fourteen ounces. We took her immediately to the NICU, and the team there is assessing her. She'll most likely be on a respirator. I think around seventy percent of babies at twenty-eight weeks gestation need some type of breathing help. It might just be a CPAP machine, but that would be the best-case scenario."

The doctor paused.

Davis said, "How is Kim?"

"She's just waking up. We had to put her completely out, so it's going to be a bit until she's awake. Once she gets wheeled into recovery, you'll be able to go back. You'll need to scrub up in order to go to the NICU, and there'll be someone in to help you with that in a bit."

"So the baby's fine, and Kim's fine, too?" He just needed to make sure that he heard all that correctly. He wasn't sure that there was anything else that he really needed to know right now.

"That's right."

"Is the prognosis good for both of them?"

"The prognosis is excellent for Kim. I'm not quite sure what caused the premature labor, but we'll keep an eye on her for a day or two. Just to make sure there's nothing else going on. The baby... She has a really good chance. Something like a ninety percent survival rate. The team from the NICU will be able to fill you in on all the details."

"All right. I appreciate it."

The doctor nodded his head, and then he said, "Is there anything else you need to know?"

Davis shook his head. Those were all the pertinent questions. Anything else could wait.

He just needed to know that Kim was going to be okay. The baby of course was important too, but the idea of losing Kim did something crazy to his insides. He couldn't stand the idea that she might be gone forever.

But if she was, he supposed he would have to deal with it. After all, whatever

God chose to give him, whatever trial he had, he needed to walk through with faith.

Still, as the doctor left, he sent prayers of thanks. Thanks for the good news so far before he began praying for their complete and total recovery.

Kim lay in her hospital bed, groggy and trying to contain her desperate need to see her baby. They would let her see her as soon as she was ready, she was sure. Fussing or throwing a fit wasn't going to make things go faster and was only going to be an annoyance to everyone.

"Dad is out in the waiting room. If you're ready, we can tell him he can come in." The nurse, who had been cleaning her up, tucked her sheets in around her and put a hand on her arm as she spoke.

She nodded immediately. "Please."

She wanted to see Davis, was suddenly desperate to talk to him. Maybe he had seen their baby. She didn't even have a name. She thought she had months to think about it, but it turned out she had been wrong.

The nurse left, and just a few minutes later, Davis showed up at the door, looking rather haggard and a bit like a desperado with the stubble on his face and the way his hair stuck up in all directions.

It made her smile.

"So I'm out there all worried, and you're in here grinning," he said as his steps slowed once he hit her doorway and walked into her room.

"I'm just happy to see you," she said, thinking that was a complete under-statement. If she had been on her feet, she would be throwing her arms around him. It was so nice to see a familiar face.

"How are you doing?" he asked, coming over and putting his hand on hers. She moved her fingers just a little and they threaded with his, and she held on tight.

He sat down in the chair next to her bed and put his other hand over them both, clasping hers between his and making her feel cared for, like a hug with their hands.

"Good, I guess. Groggy. I don't remem-ber anything. Not since shortly after we got to the hospital. But they told me she weighed about two pounds fourteen ounces, and they needed to get her set up in the NICU."

"It's a good thing this hospital has an NICU, or she'd be in a helicopter bound for Chicago right now."

"Oh. I hadn't thought about that. And here I was so impatient to see her, but I guess I should be grateful that she's still here, and I will get to see her."

"Exactly. I suppose the doctors will let you out early, if they needed to. But from what I understand, they want to keep you for a while."

"I haven't heard too much, but they haven't figured out what made her come early and just want to keep an eye on me." She felt a little sleepy, the effects of the anesthesia, or whatever they used to put her out, and maybe blood loss, she didn't know. No one told her. She didn't care. She wanted everyone's attention to be on the baby.

"Are you in any pain?" he asked gently.

She shook her head. "Not yet. They said it would probably come, but they wanted to try to stay ahead of it. I hope they do, but I just really want to get up and go see her."

"I'll stay on them, but I'm sure they'll let us back as soon as they can. I suppose I would rather they get her stable, make sure she's breathing and everything's going well, rather than making us seeing her a priority."

"Yeah. Thanks for your rational thought. I guess as a mom, all I can think is that I want to be with her, but I probably would just be in the way right now. Even though, it feels like a mom's arms is the best place for a baby."

"I agree with you there in normal circumstances." They exchanged a serious look, and then Kim closed her eyes.

"I haven't named her, but I remember from the night we met, the night we... Anyway, you mentioned that your mother's name was Kathleen. I thought that was such a pretty name. What do you think?"

She opened her eyes just in time to see the surprise on his face.

"You want to name her after my mom?" he asked, like he couldn't believe it.

"Yeah. That's her grandmother."

He nodded. Thoughtfully. Maybe thinking about some memories. She wanted to ask, but she was a little tired and a little afraid that maybe she had suggested the wrong thing. She couldn't remember all the details of what he had said, just that his mom had died of some kind of infection when he was young and that he missed her. He'd mentioned her name, and at the time, it had struck her as a pretty name, although she hadn't really been thinking about his mom, she'd been thinking more about her problems and how she just wanted to get away from them for a while.

One thing had led to another, and their baby had been conceived.

Unexpected evening all around, at least for Kim. And from what she understood from Davis, it wasn't exactly a normal evening for him either. She had to hand it to him, he certainly had been there for her. He was here now. He hadn't left, and he wasn't on the phone, wasn't taking care of his own things, but was totally focused on her.

Not that she thought he should be, but it definitely made her feel cherished in a way she never had before. Definitely not with her first husband.

"Your mother was Iva May, but that doesn't make a very good middle name.

What if we name her Iva May Kathleen and call her Kathleen?"

She wasn't sure why that brought tears to her eyes, but it did. He was being so sweetly considerate. Staying beside her, holding her hand, racing to be with her, and now, wanting to make sure that her mother was represented as much as his in the name of their child.

"I didn't mean to make you cry. I'm sorry, I didn't mean to bring your mother up. I didn't realize—"

She shook her head. "No. It's fine. It's not about my mom, it's... I'm just not used to anyone being this nice to me. Thank you."

He closed his mouth. His lips flattened out into a straight line like her words didn't make him happy, but she couldn't help it. That was the truth. She wasn't quite sure why being treated well made her want to cry, but it did. But it was crying in a good way, the kind of crying that came from happy emotions.

"Can I get you anything?" Davis asked.

"Just you being here is more than enough. Thank you," she said, squeezing his hand and closing her eyes, tired, but not wanting to miss the first opportunity to go see her baby.

"Did you see her?" she asked without opening her eyes.

"No. They haven't let me see anything. I was desperate to get to you, but I guess because your C-section was unexpected, they had put you out completely, and they made me cool my heels in the waiting room."

"Maybe they'll let us go together." She would insist on it. Surely the hospital wouldn't keep a father from seeing his daughter, any more than they would keep the mother from seeing her, as soon as she was able to be seen.

They sat there in silence for a little bit, Davis seeming to understand that she was exhausted, and not wearing her out with small talk. It was enough that he was holding her hand.

"Are you ready to see your little girl?" a cheerful voice said.

Kim opened her eyes to see a smiling, matronly-looking nurse walk into her room.

"Yes!" she said, and while her voice wasn't loud, there was definitely a whole pile of excitement in it.

"Take it easy. You don't want to make any sudden movements and pull at your staples. That's going to hurt once all of the pain meds have worn off."

"Yes, ma'am," Kim murmured, remembering that the doctor had said something to that effect. That she needed to be careful what she did. That she should expect pain. That he had to cut a lot of muscles, and it would take a while to heal.

"All right, I just want to check your vitals, and we're looking for a wheelchair for you. The NICU has told us that you can go down to see her for a few minutes.

They don't quite have her settled like they want, but they knew you were eager."

"That's great."

Davis squeezed her hand, which prompted her to say, "Can Davis go?"

"I'm sure he can. Neither one of you can stay very long, but I'm sure both of you are just dying for a little glimpse of her. She's real tiny, and you won't be able to hold her. I don't want to get your hopes up about that. They might let you touch her hand. Depending on how she's doing."

"All right," Kim said, steeling herself. She figured she wouldn't be able to hold her. That wasn't an issue. But...to not be able to touch her at all? It felt like touch was a way of communication, especially with babies who couldn't talk. But she understood that developmentally she might not be ready for skin contact. It might hurt her instead of feeling good.

She'd have to trust the doctor.

She must have drifted off, because the next thing she knew, Davis still had a hold of her hand but also gripped her shoulder gently. "Are you ready to go?"

Her eyes popped open. She couldn't believe she'd fallen back asleep with the idea of going to see her daughter so close.

"Yes." She started to struggle to get up, felt a twinge of pain, and lay back.

"Hold on. I think the bed sits up."

"It does. And you're going to want to take it easy. If you can keep the pain levels down, it'll be much better for you. Especially if you're going to be spending a good bit of time in the NICU once they get things settled."

"I'd like to spend as much time with her as I can." That was her sincere wish, but then her face clouded over as a thought occurred to her. Somehow, she was going to need to support herself. She couldn't start a new business and still be in the NICU sitting with her baby.

And she remembered the doctor saying something about Kathleen needing to stay in the hospital until a lot closer to her due date. That was three months away. How was she going to start a riding stable, doing everything that needed to be done, and still find time for her child?

It was going to be hard doing it while pregnant and with a newborn. But with the baby in a hospital in the NICU? It felt impossible.

She took a breath. She didn't have to solve that problem today. Or tomorrow. She had time.

The nurse gave directions as Davis helped her into the wheelchair. His hands were gentle, his face showing concern. He made her feel cared for, like she hadn't felt since she was very young. She loved that feeling but didn't want to take the time to enjoy it, because she was in a rush to go see her daughter.

Finally, after what felt like forever, they were rolling down the hall. She wasn't sure she would be able to follow all the twists and turns to come back.

The hospital was bigger than what she thought.

Davis and the nurse chatted a bit, although Kim didn't try to join in the conversation, just listening instead. She couldn't believe how tired she was. Her limbs felt like dead weights, and her chest felt heavy.

It was probably the effects of the anesthesia. At least she didn't feel sick in her stomach. She heard that could be a side effect as well.

"All right. Right here is the scrub station. Both of you need to take one of these little packets. When you open them, you'll find a brush and soap and you'll need to stand at the sink and follow the instructions right here." The nurse tapped a little poster that was tacked to the wall right above the sink. "Once you've done that, you have gowns to put on right here, and then you can walk to these doors and push this button. Someone will let you in. Of course, since I'm here, I'll use my badge to get us in today, but that will be the protocol when you don't have someone escorting you."

Kim assumed she was going to have to stand up from the wheelchair. She felt incredibly weak with rubbery knees and a tender middle.

Still, she would have endured a lot worse to see her daughter.

As she pushed up on the handles of the wheelchair, Davis's arms came around her gently, giving her support, helping just a bit, not enough to hurt, but steadying her, and making it so all the burden wasn't on her.

She didn't know how he knew she needed it, but she appreciated it.

She was exhausted by the time she'd scrubbed her hands clear up to her elbows for the required amount of time, put a gown and hairnet on, and was able to collapse back in the wheelchair.

Still, she couldn't contain her excitement. She had been out completely when they'd taken the baby, and she hadn't even gotten a glimpse of her.

"Ready?" the nurse said, smiling as she scanned her badge and the door started to open.

Davis looked a lot different with the hairnet and the gown, but he still had the same square jaw, the same serious but admiring eyes, the same care and concern.

"All right," the nurse said. "That group of people right there is where your little one is. We're going to hang back so we don't get in the way. They might have had a bit of a blip since the last time we spoke with them."

Whatever "a bit of a blip" was. It didn't sound good, but maybe that was the nurse's way of making it so it didn't sound terrible.

The doctors looked serious, the nurses even more so as they worked around the bassinet that Kim could barely see.

She caught a glimpse of a leg, so, so tiny.

"I have the mom and the dad, when you guys have a minute to let them take a peek," their nurse murmured to one of the nurses who were working with tape.

As the nurse backed up and turned, Kim could see her daughter, covered in tubes and wires and under a bright light, completely naked with just a diaper.

It was hard to believe that the child under all those wires was hers. Such a tiny body, so small she could barely see it.

But the thing that caught her heart and made her start to cry was when she saw that her daughter's arm was taped to a board.

Intellectually she knew that that was probably necessary to keep her from moving her arm and dislodging whatever IV they had put in there, but emotionally, to see the little arm taped to a piece of wood—tiny, but still—something to keep it straight, just tore at her heartstrings, and she couldn't keep the sob that erupted from her lungs silent.

Immediately Davis's hand was on her shoulder, going around her back, warm against the skin above her hospital gown.

"She's doing well," the nurse working on the opposite side of the incubator said, with a compassionate glance at Kim. "Mom, if you want to come a little closer, you can put your hand in this hole and touch the palm of her hand. Right now, her skin is a little sensitive, but after she grows a bit, you'll be able to touch her all over and hold her, and skin-to-skin contact will feel really good to her, and we'll encourage it. We're just trying to get her stable now, so take a couple of minutes to soak her in, she's such a beautiful, perfect baby, and then we need to keep working." The group seemed to fade back a little, to give Kim room to pull in beside her daughter.

She didn't decline the opportunity but eagerly stuck her hand through the hole, touching her baby, pushing the pain aside. Trying to, anyway.

So many things went through her head. So many questions. She wanted to know what the odds were that she would make it. She wanted to demand whether they could tell her if she was going to live or not, but she knew no one really knew. They couldn't tell her. They could give her odds, guess at percentages, but only God knew.

She wanted to ask God why? Why her? Why her daughter? Why wasn't her daughter still safely growing inside of her, but she bit down on all of those questions.

"Do you want to touch her?" she asked, withdrawing her hand and looking at

Davis. She wasn't the only parent in the room. She didn't want to take all the time for herself. Actually, she did. But that wasn't right.

Without a word, with a look of wonder on his face, he put his hand in, so much bigger than hers had been, and touched the palm of Kathleen's hand.

"I can't believe how tiny she is," he murmured. She startled at the sound of his voice, and then Kathleen seemed to settle.

"I know. I... I can't get over it. Can't get over that they're able to keep her alive."

Kathleen had some kind of thing over her nose and mouth, probably to help her breathe, and they couldn't really see her face, but her little eyes blinked once, then stayed shut.

"All right, you guys will be able to visit and stay a lot longer eventually, but for right now, we still have some work to do."

And with that, they were shooed away.

Kim didn't even make it to the door of the NICU before she was unable to hold the tears back anymore and they ran down her face. She put a finger in her mouth and bit down on it, trying to keep her sobs from erupting from her throat.

She wasn't even sure who was pushing her, didn't care, didn't pay attention to where they were going or what they were doing. Mindlessly, she took the gown they had given her off and put it in the hamper when someone told her to, swiping at her cheeks before she did so.

"I know that looks scary, but they need all those wires and tubes to make sure she gets the very best start she can. They know what they're doing, they do this every day." The nurse tried to re-assure her, and she wanted to let the nurse know that she didn't need to. Kim already knew all that, it was just… Maybe the trauma of seeing her little one, knowing that she was the mom, and having all the instincts inside of her to take care of her, but being unable to.

That, and fear.

Fear like she'd never felt before, fear of what was going to happen to her baby. Fear of what was going to happen to her.

She could hardly stand the absolute terror, sharp and hungry, that seemed to grow in her chest, and she cried harder.

Chapter 19

Davis wasn't sure what to do. Helping someone who cried wasn't exactly in his skill set. But it was Kim. And he wanted to do whatever it took to ease her pain, her fear, whatever it was.

The nurse gave him a look, and he hoped the glance he gave her in return conveyed to her that he was confident, even though he wasn't.

He wanted to ask her what he should do, but the pager at her hip buzzed, and she grabbed it, lifting it up and looking at it.

"Oh no." She swallowed. "Someone is having a baby in the parking lot." She looked at Davis, obviously wanting to take off running but knowing where her responsibility lay. "Can you get her back to her room?"

"Sure. Go on."

He couldn't believe what he was saying. He wanted to beg her to stay, to fix whatever the problem was, to do something so that Kim wasn't crying anymore. But he'd barely gotten the words out of his mouth before she had taken off, and he was left alone with the woman he loved, crying uncontrollably.

Maybe it was God, it had to be, since at that very moment he looked up, as though he was going to find some kind of help along the ceiling of the hallway, and his eyes landed on the word "chapel."

All right. If God was going to provide a chapel, he would use it.

He took the wheelchair, turning it toward where the arrow pointed and then opening the door that was clearly labeled as a "chapel." It even had stained glass windows.

Kim had quit crying, and it was almost like she had no curiosity where he was taking her, because she didn't ask where they were going. Maybe she read the door, saw the windows, but she had no reaction.

She just sniffed, her shoulders shaking in silent sobs, and she wiped at her eyes, then put her hand back down to continue to twist it in her hospital gown.

The hospital was built on a hill overlooking the lake, and big picture windows at the front of the chapel showed a gorgeous view of blue, blue water and even more blue sky, puffy white clouds, and at the very bottom there was a sandy white beach.

Beautiful place to sit and contemplate.

He pushed the wheelchair to the front of the room, praying the entire time he did so that he would have the words to say. To comfort her. To encourage her.

To ease her mind, to give her whatever she needed.

Of course, she didn't really need any-thing from him, just maybe the reassur-ance that she could look toward Jesus.

Sometimes when a person got upset, scared, or devastated, it was hard to re-member that there was a God who still loved and cared for them.

He parked her chair in front of the vast picture window, the pews and altar be-hind them. Then, he walked around, kneeling beside her, taking her cold hand into both of his, holding it gently, carefully, warming, and cradling.

"I appreciate you being here so much. I don't know what I would have done without you."

"Of course. There should be two of us, right?" He meant that there had been two of them the night Kathleen was conceived. Why shouldn't there be two of them here now? It was not fair for her to have to go through it all by herself. Plus, his heart was breaking too. Not just because of their baby, but it was so hard to see Kim like this. She deserved to be happy, smiling and carefree, laughing and loving and giving love. So much of her life had been about enduring, taking the pain, and trying to put a smile on it anyway.

"I keep wanting to ask God why? Why me? Why Kathleen? So many babies are born healthy. Why does it have to be my baby that's not?" Her voice broke a little on the last question, and she started crying again. "I want to know that she's going to be okay. I kept wanting to demand the nurses and doctors tell me that they were going to save her life, but I knew they couldn't. I just... I wanted to hear that."

He didn't say anything, just held her hand, and brought it to his lips. Wishing he could do more.

Suddenly, he decided that the wheelchair put too much distance between them, so he stood, putting his hands under her legs and behind her back and lifting her out, turning and stepping up the one step to the bottom pew where they had just as good of a view out the expansive windows, and he sat down with her on his lap.

"I'm too big for this," she protested in a watery voice, like a child protesting that they were too big to be treated like a baby anymore, but she still snuggled down against his chest, her head tucked into his chest, her arms going around him. Her sobs growing in intensity.

He didn't know what to say, so he let her cry it out. Words didn't seem like enough anyway.

He stared at the beautiful view, feeling the calm that looking at the lake always brought, thinking about how big God was. Lake Michigan was just a tiny drop in the bucket, literally, of what He had done and what He had made. What He controlled on a daily basis. Creating something as big as Lake Michigan was child's play to Him, He just spoke, and it happened. Nature obeyed Him so easily, and Davis knew Kim was right. God could keep them from going through this. He could speak and heal Kathleen that very second.

But He wasn't choosing to do that.

"Do you remember the story of David and Bathsheba in the Bible? Ever since the first pain, when I realized what was happening, when I knew that I might lose my baby, that story has been in my head."

"I remember."

"Bathsheba lost the baby."

David had lain on the floor for seven days begging God to save the baby.

Maybe that's where he should be now. Rather than holding her.

"Do you remember what David said after he found out that the baby was gone?" he asked.

She sat for a minute, still, thinking.

"I don't remember. Didn't he mourn in sackcloth and ashes or something?" she said, uncertainly, her voice hoarse from crying.

"Actually, I believe he was in sackcloth and ashes before the baby died. Once he lost the baby, he got up and said that he would see him again. So there was no point in mourning. Basically, he knew his baby was in heaven with the Lord, and there was nothing to mourn about at that point in time."

She sat still, and then she turned to him, and to his surprise, there was anger in her eyes. "Are you telling me that I should be happy if Kathleen doesn't make it?"

He shook his head immediately. "No. I was just telling you what David said. I guess, if we want the very best for our child, and we do," he said, his brows raised like he was asking her.

She nodded.

"The very best thing for them would be to grow up in Heaven with God?"

It was more of a statement, but he still looked at her like he was expecting a response. After all, if they looked at it that way, it was selfish for them to want Kathleen to live. It was better for God to take her, raise her in heaven, where she would never feel the stain of sin, never cry, never be sad or lonely, never die again.

"So we wouldn't have a child. She wouldn't go to school and have friends. She wouldn't have a family of her own someday."

"Are any of those things better than being with God?"

He was asking himself too, because he felt the same way.

"I never thought about it like that. But it's almost like me wanting her to stay is me being selfish." Kim's voice was faint, like she was working through it in her mind as she spoke.

"Let's not say that. It's natural. You're her mother. You want to be with her, that's the feeling that God gave you. Of course there are mothers who don't want to take care of their children, and that's unnatural and not right. So don't say selfish. Just... When you think about it in a different way, reframe the thought, that losing your daughter isn't really losing her, it's just God taking her back so He can raise her, then it doesn't seem so bad. Just... Still sad and hard."

She took a deep breath and blew it out, trembling a little.

He put a hand up, cupping her cheek, brushing it across her temple and ear and sliding it on the back of her neck over her hair, pulling her tight.

"Sad and hard is right. But...that gives me a whole new perspective. That maybe God wants her, and that would be better for her. Not that I want her to die, just if she does, maybe it's not as devastating as what I think."

"I think sometimes we know we can trust God, but we act like our way is better. But it's not better for Kathleen to be here than in heaven. But also, God's way is better than our way, right? Because if it were our way, this wouldn't happen. Also, I guess there must be lessons that God wants us to learn. Or experiences He wants us to experience or lives we need to touch."

She looked at him thoughtfully, the tears still on her cheeks, but she was no longer crying. "Maybe God had this happen so that you and I would spend this time together?"

"Maybe." He looked her in the eyes, her lashes still wet, but her expression sincere. "Actually, I like that idea. That God is a romantic. Although, maybe He's not quite a romantic in the way I think He's a romantic."

"I want to say that I could give Him a few pointers, but that's not true. Maybe, maybe the way character is formed amid hardship, relationships formed in hardship grow our character and grace. If we handle them right."

"Now that's a real good way of looking at it," he said, nodding his head and liking the thought. "It makes sense that hardship can grow more than just character in a person, that it can forge two people together in a relationship as they deal with the things that they need to deal with. In the right way."

They smiled together, and then she said, "I guess we just need to make sure we deal with it the right way."

"That's true. I think if we do that, we won't be the only ones who benefit. After all, people don't really notice you unless you're different. Unless you respond and act differently."

"Act like a Christian, instead of someone from the world with no hope."

"I'm sure calmness and complete assurance in the idea that God is sovereign—the ability to let go of our desires and expectations and just rest in God—knowing with a certainty that whatever happens is totally fine, is probably not an attitude that people around here see much."

"But it would be really good testimony, wouldn't it?"

He nodded. "It sure would. And maybe that's one of the things that the Lord wants from us. To take our eyes off ourselves and to put them on Him, enabling us to better notice the people around us, and how we can minister to them, instead of worrying about what's going to happen to us."

"That's a really good thought. I actually was scared earlier, because... I didn't know how I was going to start a business while I was pregnant and handle it with a newborn. I have even less idea how I'm going to do it with the baby in the NICU, because I want to be here with her. I hardly can if I have to be at home, starting a business. And I don't have anyone to fall back on."

"You have me. Please don't count me out. In fact, count me in. You have me." He repeated himself, wanting her to understand that.

"I can't expect you to do everything for me. I know you have other things to do."

"I don't. Once I have the partnership dissolved between your ex-husband and me, I'm just looking for things to do. Actually, I really enjoyed going to look at the horses with you. I was getting excited about the idea that there'd be a riding stable and horses to take care of and people coming and going and...working with you."

Her breath caught, and that thrilled his heart. That maybe she wasn't as immune to him as what he kept thinking she was. Maybe there was some hope for them after all.

She looked away, down at his shirt, where her hand rested.

"Kim. I want to. At least let me take care of the horses when they come Wednesday."

"Don't you want to be here?"

"I'll be here as much as I can. There's also the possibility that we can hire someone to help in the stable. I can put a word out, and we'll see if anyone turns up."

"I can't afford that."

"But I can. And you can consider that I'm doing it as a dad so that I will have extra time to spend at the hospital with my daughter. And you."

"I'll be out soon."

That reminded him. "I think they probably want you back in your room. They wanted to keep an eye on you."

"I know. I'm tired."

"I suppose if I don't take you back, they're going to be coming for you."

"Let them come. I think that was far better for my mental health to work through this, remembering and being reminded of the need to live out what I believe, to ease my mind, and let me know that this was something that I didn't need to worry about. Not Kathleen, since she's in God's hands, and myself or my business either, since that's in God's hands too."

"God sometimes uses people to help. That would be me. That's why I'm here."

He wanted her to admit that, wanted her to accept his help, and even if they weren't quite thinking of themselves as a team, even if they didn't have a relationship yet, he wanted to be the one she looked to, but he couldn't force it. Although, he could let her know that that was what he wanted.

"I... I hope that eventually, it might be possible for you and I to be a mom and a dad, together, for Kathleen. I'm not just saying that because I want the best for Kathleen. I'm saying that because what we did, I know it was wrong, but I don't think it was something that either one of us normally did, because there is something there between us. And if we go on the assumption that God did this partially to give you and me time to spend together, then maybe we ought to keep our eyes open to the idea that perhaps we were meant to be together."

She stayed still, staring at his shirt, not moving, but he could tell she was listening.

She had relaxed a little, wasn't nearly as tense, and no longer looked like she was ready to break. In fact, she almost looked peaceful.

"That makes sense. I guess I have trouble believing that somebody wants me—"

"I do!"

"And all the other issues, trying to trust, that we already talked about. But you're right. I can hardly sit here and say that it looks like God did this so that we would have the opportunity to spend time together and then turn my mind off to the possibility. I... I agree with you."

"Nice. You want to tell me exactly what you agree with me about?" he teased her.

But she didn't smile. "About what you said. Neither one of us normally does what we did. I know I don't, and there definitely is something about you. You... Even when you're not holding me, or giving me visions of my child in heaven that almost make me wish that we were there together, and rushing me to the hospital, and making me feel like I'm valued and wanted, even when none of that is going on, I find you...to be exactly the kind of man I've always dreamed about."

His heart stumbled, and his lips wanted to curve up into the biggest smile his face had ever seen, but he couldn't allow it to happen. Didn't want her to... Why not? Why didn't he want her to see it?

He allowed the grin that wanted to stretch his face apart to be as wide as it wanted to be.

"You have to know those words were just about the best thing I've ever heard."

"This is the weirdest place to be romantic, but I actually feel...a calm. A total peace."

"The peace that passes understanding?"

"Yeah." She had a look of wonder on her face. "I hadn't considered that, but yeah, like the peace of God has settled in my soul, and a calm assurance that everything is going to be okay. Not that Kathleen is not going to die, maybe she will, but that everything is going to be okay because God is in control."

"I've been praying for God's peace. I think He answered my prayer. I have a real good feeling about everything. Not that everything is going to be easy, but like you said, that everything's going to work out."

Chapter 20

When they got back to the room, Bill and Bev were waiting for them. Kim greeted them with a huge smile, which caused both of them to blink, look at each other, and then look back at her like they weren't quite sure what was wrong.

"I take it everything's okay?" Bev said hesitantly, like she couldn't figure out why in the world Kim would be smiling.

"It's more than okay." She glanced at Davis, who smiled back at her. They shared a little humor at the way their smiles discombobulated her parents. And how it mirrored what they'd been saying. How when people do things correctly, in a Christian manner, it oftentimes seemed unexpected, because so few people did that.

Kim said a silent prayer that she would be able to continue to have peace and trust the Lord. Then, she told her parents everything she knew, getting sleepier and sleepier as she got further into her story.

Finally, Davis suggested that he move her from her wheelchair to her bed, and she didn't protest.

To her embarrassment, she fell asleep before her parents left, but not before she saw the pastor walk in. She was pretty sure she greeted him but wasn't entirely certain when she woke up much, much later.

Davis sat in the chair beside her bed, one of his hands holding hers, his head leaning back, his mouth partially open, and small snores escaping as he breathed in and out.

She smiled. He looked a little younger in sleep. But just as devastatingly handsome.

She watched him for a bit, not moving, not wanting to awaken him. Content. Unbelievably content.

She couldn't believe that she wasn't more worried or concerned, but the conversation that she had with him was everything she needed to hear, everything she needed in order to put her trust completely in God and know that He had their very best interests at heart.

Those feelings got her through the hard days ahead as Kathleen fought for life. Her doctors were awesome, and Kim spent as much time as she could with her.

Davis didn't leave her side for the first two days, but he had to go home on Wednesday when they were getting the horses.

It was funny that he had just left when her lunch arrived, and as the aide who delivered it was leaving, Kim's phone rang.

She glanced at the caller ID before she swiped to answer.

It was Todd.

She almost didn't answer when she saw that it was him.

But while he hadn't treated her well, being unkind to him in return was not exactly what a Christian should do. She knew it, even as she wanted to ignore him or at the very least be mean. The new peace that filled her soul allowed her to almost smile as she swiped her phone.

"Hello?" She was kind of shocked that her voice sounded friendly and kind.

"Kim. It's Todd."

"I know."

Mashed potatoes steamed on the tray in front of her, along with a piece of meat, and a dinner roll which looked delicious. Her mouth watered.

"Hey, I was hoping you were getting out of the hospital today, and I thought maybe we could go somewhere for dinner?"

She blinked. Her mouth opening, then closing, then opening again. "Todd. I just had a baby."

"I know. But it's going to be in the hospital for a while. I figured I'd take you out. You know, to celebrate and all that."

"If they let me out of the hospital, I'm going to go to the NICU, and that's where I'm going to be until they kick me out."

"They won't let you stay there all night. You can come home with me. We'll get a hotel or something together."

She remembered what Davis said about how much her land was worth, and she had to believe that that was probably the only reason Todd was talking to her now. She couldn't imagine anything else. Even when they were married, he hadn't wanted to go out with her.

"If you'd like to come see me in the hospital, you may. But no thank you on the dinner. I... I just don't have time."

"You have all the time in the world. What are you going to do?"

"I'm going to spend it with my daughter."

"You can't be serious. You're just going to sit and look at a baby all day? Come on. You can spare a couple of hours to go out with me. And you're not going to sleep there anyway." He paused. "Is Davis there? Is that why you don't want to go with me?" He didn't give her a chance to answer but continued. "You know," he lowered his voice, "Davis is probably just after your land. I didn't want to tell you this while he was there the other day, but your property is worth a good bit of money. A couple hundred thousand dollars probably, and I bet Davis has his eye on it."

So he did know. And he vastly underestimated the value of her property. On purpose most likely.

She would trust Davis a long time before she would trust Todd, who had lied to her over and over again, while Davis had been nothing but considerate and completely honest.

"Thanks for letting me know. I'm sure you only have my best interest at heart." Somehow she managed to keep any trace of sarcasm out of her voice, even though she really wanted to be mean about it. Maybe he really did care about her in his own way. She highly doubted it, but she supposed she should at least try to give him the benefit of the doubt.

"Now if you don't mind, I'm kind of tired and my lunch is getting cold."

"Kim. Come on. Don't do this. Not after all the time we shared together. Surely that means something to you."

She managed not to snort. What time they'd spent together? She spent most of their marriage alone. She didn't want to think about all the time she'd been married but alone.

Still, God had been so good to her. Kind of funny that was what she was thinking as her daughter was in the NICU, but her conversation with Davis had really opened her eyes. Not just about how she should respond to her daughter and her issues and not consider questioning God, but questioning herself and what she should be doing, but also opening her eyes to how she treated people, and whether or not she was acting the way Jesus wanted her to. After all, if she was doing that, she would be very, very different from the rest of the world.

Not that she expected perfection in herself. She was never going to be that. But she could try to keep her eyes on Jesus and try to consider how she treated others, instead of being focused on how they treated her. That was certainly the way she focused when she was around Todd, easy to do with all the things that he had done to her that had hurt her and made her cry. That he'd destroyed her hopes and dreams and left her to rebuild her life alone, just when they should be settling back and enjoying their empty nest together.

God probably had some lessons for her in that too, if she'd only open her eyes long enough to see them.

But she really didn't know what to say to Todd. There was no going back. They were divorced, and that was final.

"Todd, we do have history together, but you chose to leave our marriage. And this is just the way it goes when you make a choice like that. I don't want to be mean, I don't want to be unkind, but there's never going to be anything between us. The divorce is final." She took a breath and heard him do the same, knowing he was going to argue with her. "Goodbye."

She swiped off before he could say something else. Technically, she supposed he could say she hung up on him, but she didn't do it to be unkind, she just did it so she didn't have to listen to him anymore. He wasn't taking her no for an answer, and as she thought about it, he never had. Never paid attention to what she said. He only paid attention to what he wanted.

Shoving those thoughts out of her head, she said a small prayer of thanks for her food and started eating.

Chapter 21

Rodney Southhall sat in his bedroom of the mansion his parents owned on the hill just south of the small town of Strawberry Sands.

His dad was a prominent attorney who had made millions in Chicago as a corporate lawyer, and his mom was a pharmaceutical exec.

They'd built the big mansion overlooking Lake Michigan and now commuted to Chicago, working from home as much as they both could. His mom was currently doing a video board meeting, and his dad was holed up in his office, probably writing a brief.

Rodney was bored out of his mind, because he was grounded for deliberately spiking the punch at the fancy gala his parents had insisted he attend with them the night before.

He'd gotten the whiskey from his dad's cabinet in the den, and the only fun of the evening had been seeing Mrs. Doolittle, drunk, trailing toilet paper on her shoe, as she asked everyone she ran into where her dentures were.

It was the best time he'd had in a long while and totally worth being grounded today.

He had the TV on, but he wasn't really watching it. He was just imagining what life would be like when he was finally out of the house. He hated it here. His parents were only interested in work, and they dragged him along to whatever functions they could, in order to present the illusion of being the ideal American family.

Except, instead of having two point five children, they just had one.

It used to be in the summers he'd go to his grandparents' farm in the UP, but since they both died, and their farm had been sold, he didn't even have that to look forward to anymore.

An odd noise outside the sliding glass doors caused him to lift his head off the pillow where he lay on his bed and look out.

Did he see something red moving in the bushes? Was that a bird?

He narrowed his eyes, then laid his head back down on his pillow.

Then, figuring he didn't have much to lose, he lifted himself off the bed and strode to the sliding glass door, shoving his hands into the pockets of his jeans and squaring his shoulders under his T-shirt.

His parents took his cell phone when they relegated him to his bedroom, or he might have missed the noise.

But as he looked down, he could see that there was actually movement.

And it wasn't a bird.

His dad's office was on the other side of the house, and if his mom was in a board meeting, she always had the curtains closed in hers, which was just down the hall from his bedroom, with one window looking toward the bushes where he was now staring.

The board meeting would last all afternoon.

He didn't give it much more thought but opened the sliding glass door and stepped down. He almost thought that it looked like a person. Although he wasn't afraid. It was Strawberry Sands after all. There was never anything going on. It would actually be a little exciting if it was a person and they were there to rob the house. Or... Whatever people did when they snuck around bushes.

This person was really small.

Its movement stopped as soon as he stepped out, like whoever it was had heard him open the door.

He narrowed his eyes. Maybe he should just go back into his room and pretend he never saw anything. But he didn't have anything else to do. So, he moved a little to the side so that whatever it was would end up trapped in the corner made by the two sides of the house.

The bushes shook as the red shirt moved. He could be wrong, but it looked like a kid.

"Hey, there. Stop what you're doing and look here."

"I bet," the person said, and Rodney got the idea that it was a scrawny little boy. "You don't need to call the cops. Look the other way and forget you ever saw me." The words were spit out, in a low voice, like the kid was used to running from people, being quiet, and not wanting to be seen.

"Hold up. I never said anything about the cops. Maybe I'm just as wanted as you are." Hardly. Spiking the punch was the worst thing he'd done in his entire life, and honestly, he felt like it wasn't that bad. Why were his parents upset about it? They drank alcohol at home. There was alcohol at the party. So what if one more thing had a little alcohol in it? It wasn't that big a deal.

"Whatever, Rich Boy," the kid said, and the way it said "Rich Boy" made him think that...maybe it was a girl.

He walked a little closer.

"I'm warning you. I bite. I don't have my shots."

"Me, either." A lie, since he had every single shot known to man and then some. His mother saw to that. If something new came out on the market, they jammed it in his arm.

He felt like a pincushion at times and definitely overprotected. He didn't need all those jabs.

"Whatever. Rich Boy. You probably have so many shots you could give me a drop of your blood and I'd be immune to everything for the rest of my life."

"I can hardly give you a drop of my blood when you're hiding behind the bushes. Get out here like a normal person."

"Yeah. So you can tell Mommy and Daddy and they can come cart me off. No thanks. Just look the other way, and I'll be gone."

"You hungry?" he asked, saying the only thing he could think to say. He was hungry. He had just been thinking about sneaking off to the kitchen before he'd heard the noise.

"No." The answer was short and belligerent. It was obviously meant to be a yes, but no was what their situation required.

"You come inside with me, and I'll take you to the kitchen. You eat with me, and I'll make sure you get out of here with no one seeing." This would be his entertainment for the afternoon. It might be fun to try to hide this from his parents and the gardener and the stable hands.

"I know a trap when I hear one, Rich Boy. I'm gonna make a run for it. I'm warning ya, you don't want to tangle with me. I bite. Hard. I know how to draw blood. And I know where to kick you where it hurts."

He didn't doubt it. She looked half feral. Very, very interesting.

"Where you from anyway?"

"From a nice little house downtown with a white picket fence, with a mom and dad who will be very upset if they're inconvenienced by having to deal with the police."

He bet. "You're a liar."

"You're a jerk."

"I offered you something to eat, offered to help you get out undetected, I don't understand how that makes me a jerk." He was a little offended. After all, he hadn't been anything but nice to the little twerp.

He'd barely gotten the words out when a red flash popped out of the bushes and took off alongside the house. He took three steps forward, grabbing her around the waist. Luckily, he had pinned her arms to her sides, because her feet kicked out, and she really did try to bite him.

"Don't bite me, you little brat," he said. She was smaller than he expected. But tough. Stringy small. Like she didn't get much to eat but did a lot of running or exercise or something anyway.

Of course, what did he know about girls? Especially girls this size. He knew the girls his own age were very, very interesting. A little twerp like this was more of an inconvenience. Except, he had nothing else to do.

"I won't if you let me go," she shouted in a whisper, still struggling, more frantically, the longer he held her.

"I'll feed you first, you little brat, although I don't know why. If you bite me, I'll probably lock you in the pantry for a couple of days, until your parents start looking for you. They'll be pretty upset to find you there."

"Good luck with that," she said, and he wasn't quite sure what she meant.

"Good luck with what?" he asked, pressing her as tight to him as he could, trying to get control of her legs.

"Nothing," she muttered, still struggling.

"Settle down," he said sharply.

"Let me go!"

"I'm going to feed you first, if I have to shove the food down your throat. You weigh about twenty pounds."

"I'll bite you."

"That's an idle threat. Third time, and so far, I don't have a single tooth mark on me." He probably shouldn't be tempting fate, because it wasn't like the little brat hadn't tried to bite at least sixteen times. "Stop struggling. I don't want you to hit anything when I walk in. My parents are here, and we'll both be in trouble."

"Your little rich boy butt will be in trouble, not me. Why don't you just let me go. You don't know what you're messing with."

"I know. I know. I'm messing with a wild, feral, ferocious animal that has rabies and who knows what all else, that you're going to transmit to me whenever you bite, but if you're lucky enough to break my skin and actually get a little bit of my blood, you'll get all of the immunization antibodies my rich boy butt has gotten over the years, so you'll be set for life. Now I know why you want to bite me."

"That's not how you get immunity," the girl spat out, and he grinned.

"She has a brain, does she?"

"That's why I weigh so much. Because it's so big. Let me go."

"I think you have it backward. That's why you weigh so little, because your brain's so tiny I could call you chicken brain, but it seems kind of mean to pick on someone who has so little."

"Shut up, stupid rich boy."

"Be quiet. We're going inside, and if you're loud, you're not getting anything to eat."

To his surprise, she did stop struggling when he started opening the sliding glass door, like maybe she was surprised he was actually taking her into the house, or maybe she was tired.

No, she was so tough and stringy. He'd bet she could go all day long. But her head was swiveling around. She was either amazed at what she saw in the house or looking for a way out.

"Now be quiet, and we'll sneak down the hall. The kitchen isn't far, and once we're there, we should be good."

"I'm being quiet," the girl snapped out. Her voice held irritation, but she didn't struggle.

Maybe she was waiting for him to relax his guard.

He'd tried to stay vigilant, but he also wanted to sneak past his mom's office without being heard.

"Be quiet," he said as he took the remote to his TV and turned the volume up. It wasn't much, but it was all he could do to try to drown out any sounds they made.

Keeping one arm around the girl's waist, with her arms pinned to her side, he held her off the ground while he opened his bedroom door and slid out. It was awkward trying to walk while carrying her, but he had to give her a hand, she didn't move, and she didn't make a sound.

They made it to the kitchen, and he breathed a sigh of relief which turned out to be premature, because the second the door shut behind them, she bit his arm, which made him yelp and drop her, and she took off like a shot across the floor.

He didn't worry about his dad hearing anything. Normally when his dad worked, he had eighties rock music playing, and he wouldn't notice a thing. But he couldn't have the little brat loose around the house. Not to mention, there was a full set of teeth marks, both upper and lower, in a nice circle on his forearm. She'd broken the skin with one of her incisors, and he wasn't going to let her get away with it.

He was tall for his age, and she had to stop to open the door to the kitchen on the other side since their mansion had been built with the idea that someone else would be making meals for them, and the kitchen was completely enclosed.

That's how he was able to grab hold of her, and this time, his grip wasn't nearly as gentle.

"You little brat. You bit me. I should bite you back."

"I told you I was going to. Put me down."

"Not until I get some duct tape on your mouth," he muttered. Knowing he couldn't duct tape her. If she suffocated, then he really would be in trouble.

"Shouldn't you be off getting a tan or a pedicure or something," she muttered, but there wasn't quite as much venom in her voice. He supposed she knew she'd hurt him, and the fact that he hadn't done anything in retaliation, even though she was at his mercy again, probably should be cluing her in to the fact that he wasn't going to. She might be a little beast, but she wasn't stupid.

"No. I should be doing exactly what I'm doing, which is raiding my kitchen so we have something to eat." He walked to the pantry and opened the door.

"So what do you want?" he asked as he stood inside after turning on the light.

"Water. Soda rots your guts."

"All right. Coke it is. What else?"

"You're a jerk."

"I'm feeding you. Appreciate it."

"Fine. Whatever."

He started to grab some chips, but then he figured she probably really didn't get much good food. Deciding he'd take the chips after all, because who didn't love chips even if they weren't healthy, he backed out of the pantry and went to the refrigerator. Grabbing some fruit with one hand, he held the container to her.

"Hold this."

Of course she didn't have hands, so he set her carefully down on the floor and allowed her to pull her hands out from underneath his arm, but he kept his arm around her waist.

To his surprise, she put her hands on the container and held it.

"Just hold up." He pulled out some cheese, some meat, and stacked them on top of the container of fruit. "Mayonnaise and mustard?"

"Whatever," she said, but her voice was much more subdued, and it didn't have the venom of before.

"All right. Both." He set them on top of the fruit. Then he grabbed a loaf of bread from the drawer where they kept it and a knife from the silverware drawer.

"Now, follow me," he said, like he hadn't let go of her waist and put his hand in her ragged hair.

"Let go of my head. I'm not a dog."

"You bite like one," he said, looking again at the marks on his arm which were turning purplish red, except for the few drops of blood from the place where she'd broken the skin.

"Shut up, Rich Boy." But again, her voice was much more subdued, and he could miss his guess, but he thought she was drooling. The kid must be starving.

He would've liked to take her out to the courtyard, where they could sit in the sunshine, but both his mother's office and his dad's office faced it, and while his mother's blinds would be closed, he wasn't so sure about his dad. His dad wasn't as predictable and was as liable to be sitting out there working with his music playing as he was to be in his office.

So, he carefully opened the kitchen door, walked around the corner, and started down the steps to the basement.

Chapter 22

"**W**hat? Do you have a dungeon down here or something?" the kid asked, and Rodney figured that the bravado in her voice was to hide her actual fear.

"That's right. I'm putting you with all the other brats I found out in the garden snooping around."

"Yeah. Because you're so tough," she sneered.

He ignored her, figuring she had every right to be scared and knowing she was covering it with big talk. He didn't know what her story was, but he was going to get it. He almost laughed, because if he used the food as a bribe, he was pretty sure he could get her to admit anything.

'Course, it might not be the truth. Sometimes when his parents were demanding answers from him, he told them what they wanted to hear instead of what the actual truth was.

It might be better for him to try to be her friend.

Except, he didn't want to be nice to her for pretend. He wanted to be nice for real. Whatever she was, she was filthy, skinny, and he felt bad for her. Although he was still a little mad about his arm, which hurt.

Their basement was a huge open area, with exercise machines and a home gym set up on one side complete with wall mirrors and a fridge with cold water, while on the other side was a huge flatscreen TV that took up most of the end wall, with seats and couches in front of a home theater complete with sur-round sound.

"Holy cow," the girl breathed beside him.

"And if you don't talk, I can put you on one of those ancient torture devices and make you talk," he said, referring to the exercise equipment.

"Don't be stupid, Rich Boy, I know what exercise equipment looks like."

"I wasn't sure, Brat."

"I have a name."

"I do too. It's Rodney."

"Just Rodney? You mean, rich boys only have one name?"

"Rodney Englebert Rochester Southhall the Third, if you must know." He hated his name. Hated how long and pretentious it was.

"Well, that's a mouthful. Big, fancy name. I'll just call you Dixie," she murmured.

He led her over to a chair, figuring she wasn't going anywhere until she ate now. She was holding the container in her hands, but he could remedy that easily enough.

"What's your name?" he said, taking the food from her and indicating the chair where he wanted her to sit.

She plopped on the floor instead. "Becky Peck, but you can call me Becky. I don't have a gazillion titles after my name."

"I don't have any titles after mine, either."

"Rodney Southhall, ruler of Strawberry Manor, Prince of Strawberry Sands, and King of Lake Michigan."

"You're not even funny. Now, you can make your own sandwich unless you need me to show you how. We don't eat off the floor here, and I don't have a dog bowl handy."

"Shut up, Dixie."

"Okay, Bekpek," he said, teasing her but realizing that it was probably a good name for her, especially if she was going to call him Dixie. Dixie wasn't exactly a manly name, but it was better than Rich Boy.

"Now, I'm wondering why you're sneaking around your own home, same as I am, why?" She leaned forward, like she was interrogating him, as she stared at him, which he had to admit was a little disconcerting. Especially with her teeth right below her eyes like that.

"I spiked the punch yesterday at my parents' big shindig, and Mrs. Doolittle got drunk, ran around with toilet paper stuck to her shoe, and asked everybody where her dentures were. So, what's the story with you?"

She snorted, and he figured he did the right thing by telling the truth. Even if it was embarrassing. After all, he hadn't meant to make anyone make a fool of themselves.

"I just sneak around houses for the kicks and giggles," she said.

He figured he wasn't going to get the accurate story from her. Not until she trusted him. Which she probably wasn't going to do today.

"How old are you?"

"Thirteen."

"So you're ten."

"Eleven."

That was probably pretty accurate.

"Do your parents know you're here?"

"Of course." She already had two pieces of bread, and she'd slapped enough meat on them to make three sandwiches and enough cheese that it made his stomach roll.

"You can have more than one sandwich," he said, lifting a brow at the monstrosity that she held in both hands.

She took a bite and then spoke with her mouth full. "Whatever, Dixie."

At least that's what he thought she said.

"So, what's your story?"

She chewed, thankfully, although her mouth was open half the time. But he supposed this wasn't the time to insist on proper table manners. Not that he really cared, since he didn't. It was just that it had been drummed into him, and he assumed that they'd been drummed into everyone else in the world as well, but this kid didn't have any.

"I don't want to talk about it," she said.

"So you were snooping around here, trying to find food. Is your family too poor to buy any?"

"No. Everyone could buy food." She rolled her eyes.

He didn't say anything else, unsure as to what her story could really be. He didn't really need to know. Although, if she was homeless, he should probably report her. She fought so hard, seemed so independent, even though she was so young. Maybe, he could deal with her without getting the full story.

"You want a job?"

"I don't do drugs. I'm not doing...other stuff."

"Oh. Other stuff?" He was pretty sure he knew what she meant, and that thought hadn't crossed his mind. Not with the skinny little girl that she was.

"I'm not taking my clothes off." She glared at him, her eyes narrow, angry.

It made him a little angry, that she'd even have to say that. Not angry at her, angry at whatever happened to her that would make her think that that would be what he would want.

"I just know where there might be a job. Thought you might want to work and earn your keep."

"I'm not doing your dirty work for you, Dixie. Rich Boy."

"Do you like horses?" Most girls did. He figured she probably would as well.

She lifted her shoulder, but he didn't miss the look of interest in her eyes. She took another bite of the sandwich, still acting like she'd been famished and hadn't eaten for a week.

"I guess they're okay," she said with her mouth full.

"We don't have to have this conversation before you swallow."

"You want me to eat, or do you want me to talk?"

"Eat first, then we'll talk." She finished that sandwich, and he didn't say anything until she started making a second one. He had no idea where she was going to put it, the first sandwich had been every bit as big as her stomach and then some.

"At the party that I had to go to yesterday, I overheard some people talking about a horse rental facility that was opening up."

"So?"

"Well, the people who are running it have a kid in the hospital, and neighbors have been helping them. I bet, if you go down there and talk to one of them, they'll hire you."

"I'm too young."

"How about if I go down with you." He was pretty sure he could sweet-talk them into giving her a job. "I'd have to say you were my sister."

"That's lying. I don't do that kind of crap."

Okay. That was interesting. Certainly un-expected.

She was eating again, so he had some time to think. His arm was burning, and his eyes fell on that. The teeth marks had swollen into a deep purple color.

The blood had dried at the end and where her incisor had pierced his skin.

That gave him an idea.

"Have you ever heard of blood brothers?" It wasn't something he ever heard anyone doing. He just read it in books, but it might be worth a shot.

"Blood brothers? Like, where you cut your hand and someone else cuts theirs, and you push them together and exchange blood?" She had stopped what she was doing long enough to look up at him, like she wasn't quite getting what he was saying.

"Yeah. That's exactly right. If you and I do that, we wouldn't be blood brothers, since you're a girl. You'd be my sister."

Her brows went up, and he could tell she was interested, then she looked at her sandwich, as though sizing it up, but he figured she was thinking.

He supposed it shouldn't matter to him whether she agreed to it or not. But he found himself hoping she took him up on it. After all, he didn't want her to have to lie, and it would be a lot easier to get her a job if he claimed she was his sister. He could clean her up, and they could make it look like she just loved horses and wanted a job.

He wasn't sure why he was so all fired set on helping her, but he realized he was holding his breath as she thought.

"I guess that would work," she said slowly, then she shrugged. "But I'm not lying."

"You didn't have a problem lying to me about your age."

"That's different," she snapped, taking a big bite of her sandwich, bigger than necessary, like stuffing her mouth full was going to get around having to explain why she lied to him.

"That's different. So lying to me is one thing, but lying to...anyone else isn't okay?"

"That's right, Dixie. Because you're a rich boy."

"Oh. And you're Robin Hood."

"I can't stand thieves."

"Really? So you were hiding around the bushes, wandering around my house, because you were studying architecture?"

"Shut up."

"That seems to be a favorite phrase of yours. Did it ever occur to you that maybe if you want to have a good argument, rather than trying to shut up the other side, you should have facts and examples to back up your position? And if you can't out-argue the other side, maybe... Just maybe, that means they're right."

He thought she was going to tell him to shut up again, but she took another bite of her sandwich instead.

He didn't need her to tell him that he was right to know that he was. A lot of people didn't want to hear the other side, because they couldn't win an argument, so they focused on shutting them up instead. Sadly, some people were so brainwashed into thinking that their side was right, despite the fact that they couldn't defend their position, that they never thought to actually hold their beliefs up to logic to see if they held water.

Maybe, if nothing else, he'd teach the little brat that before she left. After all, there was no guarantee that she would follow him down to the beach and actually ask for a job at the stable.

He realized that there was no guarantee that she would actually do her job at the stable or even show up for it.

He wasn't sure whether he wanted to put his name on the line for her like that. Strawberry Sands was a small town. Even though his family was new, there was still the potential that the people he would be going to see would recognize him and know that he was an only child.

He still thought they might get away with it because yesterday when he'd heard the people talking, they had said that the stable owners were new residents in Strawberry Sands.

Maybe they wouldn't know about the people who lived in the mansion on the hill.

He could hope.

"Why do you want me to have a job?" the girl finally thought to ask.

"Well, Bekpek, I kind of figured you like horses. I also kinda figured that you wouldn't be sneaking around my house if you had money to buy whatever it was you were looking to steal."

He said that deliberately, because he knew it would irritate her. Sure enough, thunderclouds entered her eyes, and she opened her mouth, but before she said anything, she snapped it closed. After all, they'd already established the fact that her telling him to shut up wasn't a logical argument, and as he figured, she didn't have a logical argument.

She ate the rest of her sandwich with gusto. And chewed with her mouth open.

"I can't figure out whether you actually have no table manners, or whether you're chewing with your mouth open and eating like a pig on purpose, just to irritate me."

"It's just to irritate you, Dixie." She smirked at him, and he couldn't help it, he grinned, since she talked with her mouth full again.

"You're wasting your time, because it doesn't irritate me. Actually, that's how I used to eat when I was two, too."

"I'm not two. I told you I was thirteen."

He snorted. "I'm still not convinced you're not ten."

"Ya gonna turn me in?" she asked. She swallowed the last bit of her sandwich and cracked the Coke open.

He'd brought water down too, and he smiled as he looked at it deliberately then back up at her. She'd chosen Coke over water.

She lifted her nose at him and didn't say anything as she drank in big gulps while he considered her question.

"I don't know. Why shouldn't I?"

"Because I trusted you."

"You didn't. I grabbed a hold of you and forced you to come down here with me. Otherwise, you'd be halfway to Mars by now."

"If only," she burst out.

He thought that was probably the first real words she'd said.

So she didn't like where she was, and she wanted to be away?

"Then why don't you go?"

"To Mars?" she asked with one eyebrow cocked.

"Anywhere. Why are you here?"

She kept her mouth closed and looked at him with her eyes narrowed, as though she were judging him. Maybe she found him wanting, because instead of telling him, she just shrugged her shoulders.

Fine, if that's the way she wanted, that's the way it could be. Maybe someday she'd tell him the truth.

"You didn't eat any chips. What, are you allergic to potato chips or something?"

"Bag's not open. I didn't know they were for me."

He took the bag, opened it, and set it down in front of her.

She took a handful, started munching, still looking at him like she didn't trust him.

"When you finish those, we're going to take you to get you cleaned up a little. We can't take too long, because I only have another hour and a half, or maybe two, until my parents come to my room and call me for supper. So, we can't dawdle."

"You're the one that's dawdling. And you just opened a bag of chips." She spoke, and chips flew everywhere.

He took a finger and gingerly wiped the sloppy, half-chewed chips off his arm.

"I'm not the one shoving them in my mouth." He gave her an irritated look. "I don't mind if you talk with your mouth full, but point your head that way, so you spew the crap in your mouth away from me, not on me."

"Oh. The rich boy doesn't like to get his fancy clothes all gooped up."

"I don't like having your slobbery food all over me. That's normal human behavior. If you hadn't been raised by wolves, you'd know that."

She snapped her mouth closed and turned her head away, shoving more chips in before taking another long drink of her Coke.

He hadn't meant to hurt her feelings, but he had the feeling that he had.

Chapter 23

"Thanks a lot for bringing them out and thanks for the hay contact." Davis shook the hand of the man who had delivered the horses.

They'd come off the trailer without a problem, which suited Davis just fine. Even the little Arabian mare that could barely stand had been just as sweet as could be.

He would have thought, after the abuse that she'd obviously been through, that she'd be scared and upset, possibly biting and kicking in defense, but she wasn't.

He wished Kim could be there to see the horses' heads hanging out over the edges of their stalls and smell the way the stable smelled, which was different than when it was empty.

"No problem. Go ahead and just tell him I sent you. If he's got hay to sell, he'll be happy to hear from you."

"And I'll be happy to get in touch with him." Davis nodded at the man, who lifted a hand, then turned and strode toward his pickup.

They had some hay in the barn, but Davis would really like to have it down at the stable, where it would be easier to feed. Especially during this time where he would be trying to spend as much time at the NICU with Kathleen and Kim as he could.

While he was thinking about it, he figured he would dial the number and talk to the man about hay.

He strode through the stable as the phone rang in his ear, looking at the horses, petting wide foreheads, and smiling at the thought of what Kim would do when she saw them. She was going to be so happy. It felt like her business really was getting started.

"Hello."

"Hello. I was told that you had horse hay for sale."

He wanted to explain where he lived, but he wasn't sure how to describe his relationship with Kim. He wanted to be able to say my wife and I, but even though she technically agreed that they might pursue the idea of a relationship, he was far from being married to her.

"You called the right guy, because I've got a bunch, and I'm getting ready to make more. I'd love to sell some."

They talked about price and deliveries, and the man agreed to be there the next afternoon. Davis assured him that he would help unload.

It had been years since he'd thrown hay bales around, but he had to admit he was kind of looking forward to it. If Kim were out of the hospital, along with

Kathleen, he'd almost say he would be perfectly happy.

He felt almost completely content as he scratched the head of the skinny mare. He wanted to think of a name for all of the horses, but he wouldn't name them without Kim. So, he took pictures and sent them to her.

She was focused on Kathleen, and he understood that, but he thought this might get her mind off of the what ifs and all of the other medical jargon that they seemed to get into every day.

Still, Kim had seemed totally calm and at peace ever since they talked, and it was something that he thanked God for on a daily basis, that she wasn't scared and crying. That had been one of the worst times of his life. Feeling helpless to do anything to help her feel better.

He only had one horse left to feed when he looked up to see two figures standing in the opening of the stable.

"Hey there," he greeted them, one tall and one smaller. They were not holding hands, but they were obviously together. An older brother with his little sister maybe? He squinted, but the sunlight was behind their backs and they were in shadow.

"Good afternoon, mister. We're here because we heard there might be a job available." The taller figure spoke. A boy. A young teenager it looked like, maybe fourteen or sixteen.

"Come on in here where I can see you," he invited, trying to sound friendly but not too friendly. He wanted someone who was responsible, not someone who was going to let the horses starve if he had to go to the NICU and couldn't get away.

"I'm Rodney, and this is my sister, Becky."

It was a little odd the way Rodney seemed to stumble over the word "sister." But his face looked sincere, and Becky didn't seem surprised to hear herself called his sister, so maybe he just tripped over his tongue. Sometimes Davis did that.

He closed the distance between them with his hand out. "I'm Davis. I'm pleased to meet you," he said as the kid stuck his hand out and shook, looking Davis in the eye, which Davis had to admit impressed him.

He held his hand out to Becky, who didn't shake with quite as much confidence. But she was a good bit younger if he had to make a guess. Although, it was hard to tell, since her eyes looked wise. Maybe twelve?

"Which one of you wants the job?"

"Both of us for now. But it's my sister who's really interested in horses." Rodney spoke like he was used to talking to adults, with the confidence and assurance that made Davis almost feel like maybe he grew up with money. It was an odd feeling. Because Strawberry Sands was rather small and less affluent, and all the wealthy people pretty much lived around Blueberry Beach.

"You live right in town?" he asked, thinking about the few houses that lined Main Street and a couple more that sat on a back alley. If there were fifteen houses total in Strawberry Sands, he'd be surprised.

The boy hesitated, then he shook his head. "Just a little outside of town, but it's an easy walk down the beach, and both of us are good workers. Becky especially loves horses, and she'll do pretty much anything to be able to spend time around them."

Davis wanted to go back and ask again where they lived; after all, it was a small town and he probably knew their parents, knew of their parents, or knew someone who knew their parents.

Something seemed a little fishy to him, but as he looked in the boy's eyes, he seemed like an honest kid. But it was the girl that really struck him. He could see Kim falling in love with her. She looked a little bit standoffish, and she had her arms crossed over her chest like she was trying to be tough, but she also had a desperation about her that made Davis think that she really wanted the job. Needed it. Or else was just desperately in love with horses and would do anything to be around them. He knew girls like that. Back when he was in school. Vaguely remembered ones who loved horses as much as he loved dinosaurs and Mars.

Of course, he'd outgrown that, and Becky probably would too, but it was always better to have someone doing a job they loved rather than have someone doing it who would rather be doing something else.

"Do either of you have any experience with horses?" he asked. It felt like an obvious question. Although he supposed that they didn't have to. It wasn't like it took a lot of education in order to take care of them.

"I have some. I've ridden a bit. And Becky's a fast learner. Aren't you, Bekpek?"

The little girl glared up at the boy like he used the nickname that she hated.

But then she turned to him and said, "I'm a hard worker, mister. I know a little, but I'll do whatever you want me to do, and I'm always on time. And I'm responsible. You can trust me."

Interesting that that was the angle that she took. Like him trusting her was important.

He pursed his lips, knowing he was going to hire them but just feeling like everything wasn't quite the way it seemed, but unable to put his finger on exactly what was wrong.

"All right. You actually have perfect timing because the horses just arrived today. I can show you what I'm planning to do, and we can go from there. How much are you going to charge me?"

He smiled when the little girl's eyes got wide, and she looked up at her big brother, questions in her eyes.

He gave her a little smile, almost like he was saying "I told you so," and then his head nodded just a bit toward Davis like he was telling her to look at him and tell him what she wanted.

"Whatever you give me!" she said.

"Becky means that she'll work for minimum wage, or if you'd rather just pay a certain amount every week so nobody has to keep track of hours, that would be fine too."

The boy had a little bit of a head on his shoulders, which impressed Davis.

"All right. I'm hiring both of you, right?" he said, wanting to confirm what the boy had said earlier. After all, it seemed like Becky was the one who was the most interested in the job, but she seemed a little young.

"For now. If we get to the point where you think that Becky will work out by herself, you can let me know. Not that I don't want the job, it's just that Becky would like to do it all."

"I see. I'll keep that in mind. For now, I won't be around much, because my daughter's in the NICU at the Blueberry Beach Hospital. Do you guys think you can start right away?"

"We sure can!" the girl said, looking like she wanted to pick a pitchfork up that very second.

"All right." He started talking about where the feed was, explaining that the horses didn't have names, and discussed the times that he expected them to be there. He really didn't have specific times, but he wanted the kids to do it around school.

He got things settled, and the kids worked with him for a bit before they finished up. They finalized the details and discussed when they'd be back, then he watched as the kids walked down the beach.

He made a note to himself that he wanted to walk down himself and see what kind of houses were down there. He hadn't realized that anyone lived in that direction. Not for miles anyway. And there was just something nagging about the kids. Maybe if Kim and Kathleen weren't in the hospital, he would follow up on it right away, but as it was, he went in, took a shower, threw clothes from the washer into the dryer, putting more in the washer before he texted Kim that he was on his way to the hospital, asking if she wanted him to bring anything.

The doctors had said that she would probably be released today, and he knew she was feeling more pain. He wished there was something he could do to help, but he knew it was just going to take time for her to heal.

She texted back that there was nothing, and he smiled, eager to go see her.

Chapter 24

Kim carefully handed Kathleen back to the NICU nurse. After almost a week of this, she was getting to be an expert at untangling herself from the wires and tubes and making sure they didn't get caught on anything.

She still was only allowed a limited amount of time to hold Kathleen, but she ate up every second.

Davis, waiting for her in the hospital cafeteria, hadn't been around any time that they'd been allowed to hold her. Today, he hadn't even come up because the NICU was buzzing with people since they'd gotten several babies in a short amount of time. When he called earlier, and she told him what the place looked like, he suggested that he'd come up later, just to keep the extra people down to a minimum, and be considerate of the nurses and doctors trying hard to save other people's children's lives.

"She's doing really well today, unlike yesterday." The nurse lifted her eyes as Kim shared a glance with her.

Kathleen had been restless and irritable all day the day before. But thankfully, especially since today was so busy, she had been much calmer and had slept soundly most of the day. Kim had learned in the short week she'd been there that things were usually touch and go - she had good days and not so good days.

The staff preferred not to move her much, since it affected her blood pressure and other vitals, but they also acknowledged that the bond between a mom and baby needed to be fostered, and that children responded best to their parents' touch.

"Maybe things will calm down here in a little bit, and daddy can come up and hold her." The nurse, Glenda, had been assigned to their area of the NICU almost every day Kim had been there, and they started to get to know each other well. Glenda had seen how Davis had come and cared for her.

"He would love that," Kim said, knowing it was absolutely true. Davis couldn't have been any better. Taking care of Kim, doing her laundry, making sure she ate, helping her, as the pain from her C-section limited her movements, and just generally making sure she got enough rest, and didn't overdo it. He basically took care of everything so that all she had to think about was healing for herself and caring for Kathleen.

As she walked slowly out of the NICU, the pain from her C-section still bothering her, tears pricked her eyes as she thought about how much more difficult it would have been if Davis hadn't been so amazing.

It was like he dropped his entire life and picked up hers.

As she walked into the cafeteria she could see him sitting at a table, using his laptop to work on the website that he had started for the riding stables not long after Kathleen was born. That's what he did in his free time, when he was at the hospital, with nothing to do other than sit and look at the baby who, at first they weren't even sure whether she would live or die. Davis had been there, encouraging, supportive, helpful and completely content to occupy himself when they couldn't do anything but look at the baby.

Kim hadn't even asked him to do a website. He'd just done it.

"How's it coming?" she asked, her voice causing his head to jerk up in surprise. He saw her and stood, walking toward her, leaving his laptop on the table.

He greeted her with a hug, which she returned. She'd come to lean on him, couldn't imagine doing this without him, had leaned on him heavily in the short week Kathleen had been alive.

"It's going well. You caught me at the perfect time. I just hit 'preview.' But, how's Kathleen?" he asked, knowing she was doing better today than she had done yesterday, but he hadn't talked to Kim for several hours, and they'd been doing it long enough to know that Kathleen's condition could change hour by hour, even minute by minute.

"She's doing much better than yesterday, still. Glenda is her nurse, and you know Glenda. She's amazing."

"It's funny how the nurses come to feel like family here."

Kim nodded, appreciating the fact that Davis, while not being chummy with the nurses, valued them, and saw how well they did their job.

He wasn't a flirt, and she never felt like he catered to the nurses or anything, he was just... Perfect. He showed perfectly that she was the most important one to him, while still giving the nurses deference. She didn't know how he did it, but he made her feel like she was special, but didn't make anyone else feel like they weren't.

"Glenda said as things settled down, and you made it back up, that maybe they'd find time for you to hold her. I told her you would love that."

"I sure would," he said, and she could hear the deep desire in his voice. It had been hard for her the first few days when she hadn't been allowed to hold her baby.

Somehow, Davis had just missed the opportunities. Mostly because he'd been busy taking care of the horses, washing her clothes, and making sure she ate while taking care of her home, her farm and herself.

"You look exhausted," he said, gently putting his arm around her and walking slowly toward the table where he pulled out a chair for her.

"I am. It's been such a roller coaster ride." There had been a few touchy moments where Kathleen had been in a precarious position. But the doctors have been great, and Kathleen had pulled through. Kim felt the prayers of Bill and Bev especially, but the whole town of Blueberry Beach, and also of Strawberry Sands, seemed to be praying for her. The pastor had visited several times, and Kim just felt like she was in really good hands.

"Maybe you can rest in that room they let you use?" Davis asked with his brows lifted.

"You know, I want to refuse, because I don't want to leave Kathleen for more than the time it takes to eat, but…" She sighed, the sound seeming to come the whole way from her soul, she was just so tired. "If you don't mind, I think I would like to lie down for a bit."

"I don't mind at all. In fact, I'd love to spend the afternoon with Kathleen. I'll text the social worker now, and see if the room is available." He pulled his phone out of his pocket and sent off a quick text.

Kim sighed again how well he had been taking care of her, and how much she appreciated it. He didn't miss anything. Not her tiredness, not her discourage-ment, not her pain. It was like he was attuned to every little part of her, and wanted to make her as comfortable and happy as possible. She'd never been with someone like that before.

Well, she'd spent one night with some-one like that.

She looked down at her lap. It had been wrong, but the way he'd been that night, had been the way he was all the time.

She would have thought after a week he would be tired of catering to her every need, but if anything, he'd gotten to know her better, and hadn't had to ask her what she wanted. He could just take a look at her face and know.

"I ordered your usual, but if you'd like something else?" he asked as the cafeteria workers called the number that sat on their table.

"That's perfect." He probably got her a drink too, non-caffeinated, because she was pumping. The doctors had said that if everything went well, they might start trying to feed Kathleen in another week or two. They had said that there were certain benchmarks that every baby seemed to hit at a certain time, but there were also wide variations, and no two babies were exactly alike. They just let the babies tell them when they were ready for certain things.

That made Kim feel really happy, that they were paying so much attention to how Kathleen was doing, and not forcing her to adhere to a rigid schedule that she wasn't ready for. But it was also frustrating, because she had no timeline, and didn't have any way of knowing when something would or wouldn't happen.

Davis was back shortly with their food. He set her soup and salad in front of her, and opened her drink for her.

"How are your stitches feeling? Your pain level is good?" he asked, settling himself down in the chair, and moving his laptop to where they could look at it without getting any food on it.

"It's starting to fade. The first few days were the worst, and they went by in a blur, but now, I have times where it doesn't hurt at all. That makes me want to not move."

"I bet."

That's why he opened her drink for her. Because even doing something little like that gave her pain. She probably should do something for herself, although if it were up to Davis, she wouldn't be doing anything.

They bowed their heads and he said a short prayer. He always mentioned Kathleen, and, what really impressed her was that he thanked God for caring for her, every time, before he asked God for continued care. It was something that seemed to be a hallmark of Davis. Showing appreciation before he asked for more.

It had convicted Kim more than once, since she often just sent bullet prayers to the Lord, asking for more and more and more.

"All right, if you don't mind, I can show you the website while you eat."

"I don't mind at all," Kim said, noticing the stubble on his face, and the bit of shadow under his eyes. He was tired too.

Maybe she was allowing him to do too much?

He talked about the site, showed the pictures he had up of the horses, and scrolled through the pages he made, including the schedule, which was all automated, and connected to both of their phones, as well as the waivers the riders had to sign, hours for the stable, along with his personal cell phone number in case people were interested in sunrise or sunset rides.

They would offer them. They just weren't going to open at those times. They had to be scheduled in advance.

"It seems like you thought of everything. I can't think of a single thing to improve on that. This is amazing."

"I have to thank Matt Landry. He is the one that's been bringing our hay and lives just a short walk up the beach. He and his family have a riding stable as well, and he showed me their website, told me to copy whatever I wanted. Our horses are a little bit calmer than his, and are more suitable for beginners. But other than that, and the fact that they have a bed-and-breakfast right on their farm, we're very similar in our businesses."

"That was awfully nice of him. Maybe I'll get to meet him when Kathleen gets out."

"Or, if you go home to take a shower or whatever. He's around a good bit, delivering hay. I told him he could fill up the barn."

"How much is that going to cost?" Kim asked before she could stop herself. She didn't want to think about finances right now. She had enough to worry about with Kathleen, and her own recovery.

"Don't worry about it." Davis's voice was gentle, but firm.

She looked into his eyes, so deep and blue, and felt sweet peace settle down into her heart. He had made sure that there was absolutely nothing for her to worry about, other than herself, and taking care of her baby. She didn't know how she was going to make this up to him, but she needed to.

"You've been so good to me," she breathed. "I don't deserve how good you're being."

He put a hand over top of hers on the table, and squeezed gently.

"You deserve all of that and far more."

"I don't know how I'm going to make it up to you."

"Just letting me take care of you while you take care of our baby, allowing me to take care of the farm, just allowing me a little bit of access to your life is all that I want." A slow grin. "Maybe that's not all I want, but it's enough for now."

She couldn't help but smile back at that grin, as his words thrilled her heart. Although, they scared her a little, too. Todd hadn't felt like she was enough. Hadn't felt like she was worth doing anything for. It scared her to think that maybe Davis would finally see whatever it was the Todd saw, and realize that she wasn't worth all this effort. That it was all wasted or something.

"What? You look sad." Concern entered his eyes. "Did I do something wrong?"

"No. You're doing everything right, and that's a little scary. No one's ever treated me like this before."

"Maybe you just haven't been around the right people. Don't forget, Todd's a jerk. He never treats anyone well. You deserve so much better than him. Just... Let someone take care of you. Let some-one...love you."

She sucked in a breath. That was too much.

She cleared her throat and pulled her hand away, picking up her fork like she just remembered that she was raven-ously hungry, even though she really wasn't. She'd been forcing herself to eat for several days, just because she knew that was what she needed to do in order to keep her milk production up.

"The website looks great. Is it live?" she asked, after looking around at whatever she could find to take the attention off of her and whatever lay between them. It was scary. And she wasn't used to all of those emotions swirling around her.

With Todd, it was her doing all of the effort to keep their relationship together. She wasn't quite sure how to act when there were two people in a relationship, instead of just her.

"I scared you," he said, not sounding upset or annoyed, just...making a statement of fact.

"You did. I'm sorry. I...am acting like a child who doesn't know what to say.

Probably because I don't." There, she was as honest as she could be. After all, that was part of the problem with her relationship with Todd. He hadn't been honest. Although, that was probably just the tip of the iceberg. Because, he hadn't cared, and that was a dealbreaker too.

"You're not acting like a child. I think, coming from a relationship where you aren't considered important, it's a natural reaction. But, that doesn't mean I can't consider you important, or act like you are."

"I think it's the actions that are getting me. I'm used to Todd telling me that I'm important, but his actions always said something completely different. After all, how important can I be when he never follows through?"

"I will follow through. I'll do more than follow through. But, I'm not just doing these things to convince you that you need to be with me, or butter you up, or whatever it is. I'm doing it because... Because I care, and I can't imagine not doing these things, saying that I care, and not doing everything I can to show you that I mean it."

"I know. I never thought that you were just doing them. In fact, I had been thinking that you are doing the exact same thing now that you were doing a week ago, and it hasn't gotten old for you."

"It hasn't."

"You look tired too."

"I go home every night and get a good night's rest. You've been sleeping in a hospital, and I know you're slipping into the NICU when you should be sleeping."

"They're not going to be letting me use that room beside the NICU much longer. The social worker said a couple more days and they were going to need it for someone else."

"We'll take advantage of it as long as we can. And then we'll start driving to and from the hospital, it's not that far, and we'll settle into a new routine."

"I can't ask you to drive me to and from the hospital."

"I'm offering. I want to. I'm pretty much demanding that you let me."

She smiled, because he was doing anything but demanding.

He took care of her, and acted like she mattered to him. She felt cherished. If she wasn't careful, she was going to fall in love with him. That scared her.

<h1 style="text-align:center">Chapter 25</h1>

avis walked to the garbage can and came back to the table in time to give Kim a hand standing to her feet. He tried to be gentle. He couldn't imagine having his stomach muscles cut in two, and then trying to deal with the healing as everything grew back together.

She looked exhausted, but at least she didn't look worried. He tried to take all of the things that could possibly worry her off of her shoulders and deal with them himself, while not ramroding her into anything. He didn't want to take over her business, or take over the farm. He just wanted to take over the worry.

He wasn't sure exactly how well he was doing, but that had been his goal.

Taking his computer, and shoving it back into his case, he slung it over his shoulder, putting a gentle arm around Kim, and leading her back to the elevator which would take her to the NICU floor. That's where the room was where she'd been staying off and on.

"The social worker said it was going to be okay. And she said it would be fine for the next two nights," he said, relaying the message that had dinged into his phone not that long ago.

"All right. I guess we'll just take it one day at a time. When we started out, they said one or two days, and it's been a week."

"God's been good."

"He sure has," she said, softly, but with real feeling. He echoed that. God had been better to them than they deserved, for sure. Especially considering the origins of how Kathleen had come to be.

But, whether it was because they both admitted that what they had done was wrong, or whether it was just because of God's great mercy that they didn't deserve, everything had been going so well.

Although, he'd feel a lot better when Kim didn't hurt anymore and when she didn't look exhausted.

"I really would like to go hold Kathleen. Or at least sit with her. It makes me sad to think that she's there by herself, with no one who loves her near. As good as the nurses are, she needs family."

"I'll sit with her while you sleep. Let me get you tucked in first. After all, I want to take care of both of you."

She gave him a smile, and the look on her face made him feel like she wanted to take care of him too, but she was just overwhelmed. He wanted to tell her not to worry about it, but he didn't want to be presumptuous, and he also didn't want to get into any conversation that made her withdrawn and sad.

He wanted to throttle Todd more than once for the things that he had done to her, but of course, he had to swallow that urge every time it came.

God loved Todd, just as much as he loved Davis, Kim, and Kathleen. The man just needed to... Davis didn't even know. He supposed he didn't care either, as long as he left Kim alone.

They got to the room, and Davis pulled the blinds while Kim went to the restroom.

There was a detached bathroom with a shower, as well as a bed that wasn't the most comfortable thing anyone had ever slept on, but it worked. The NICU was just a thirty second walk away, and this room was positioned perfectly for them.

She came back out, her hand on her stomach.

"Is it time for your pills?" he asked.

"I think so."

He reached into his bag, pulling them out and handed her one, then pulled out the drink that she hadn't quite finished and gave that to her as well.

He was glad she was taking the pills, because he was pretty sure one of the side effects was that they made her drowsy, and he'd like for her to get as much sleep as she could.

She lay down, and he tucked the sheets under her, her eyes closing immediately, as she curled a little around her stomach, one hand on it like she could keep the pain in by pressing.

He put a gentle hand on her back, rubbing circles as softly as he could, trying to soothe out some of the stress and worry.

"Thank you," she murmured sleepily. He didn't say anything in return. It wasn't long before her even breath told him she was asleep, or close to it. He waited just a bit longer, continuing to stroke light circles until he was pretty sure that his opening and closing the door would not wake her.

It was a heavy door, like most doors in the hospital, but at least the hinges didn't creak, and he was able to get out without making too much noise.

There was no key, and no lock, but she'd been sleeping there every night since she had the baby so he didn't worry about it as he walked down the hall to the area where he scrubbed to go into the NICU.

It was just a few minutes later when he stood in the doorway. He assumed things had calmed down since earlier, since there were no clusters of doctors and nurses, no alarms going off, and no crying parents in the corner, with a nurse or social worker standing beside them, hands on their shoulders, trying to comfort them.

He'd seen that more than once in his time here and had selfishly prayed every time that it would never be Kim and him crying over their baby.

He walked to Kathleen's bassinet, looking at her sleeping form, and sitting down beside her. He hadn't brought his computer or anything to do. When he was with Kathleen, he tried to give her his full attention, even if she slept the whole time. He didn't really see the point in just sitting there and ignoring her. Maybe if he got to spend all day every day with her it would be different.

He'd been there for thirty minutes or so when Glenda came around.

"Dad, good to see you. Would you like to hold her?" she said in greeting.

She couldn't have said anything to make him happier.

"I'd love to."

"Let me get you a chair. One that lets you lean back a little, and if you want to put her against your skin, that would probably be the way she would like it best."

He unbuttoned his shirt, and was ready when Glenda brought a chair that seemed to be designed for the purpose of parents holding their babies and leaning back with them.

"You sit here. I'll get her out, and I'll just set her down on your chest. Hopefully she'll stay asleep, and she'll just be snuggled up next to your heart."

That sounded good to Davis, and he nodded, trying not to look too eager. He couldn't remember the last time he'd been this excited, this happy, over something.

He was finally going to get to hold his daughter. Kim's daughter. Their daughter together.

He couldn't believe it. It felt surreal when Glenda laid the tiny, light, delicate little bundle in his arms. On her back, next to his skin.

"All right, I'm going to leave you here. If you need anything, you can press the button right there, okay?" She looked at him. "Don't try to put her back in yourself. Let me come get her."

"Yes, ma'am," he said, never taking his eyes off Kathleen. She was so tiny. So delicate. So precious.

He couldn't help but be overwhelmed, and he didn't want to look up because Glenda would see the tears that were pooling in his eyes. He wanted to do everything he could to fight for this little one, but all he could do was pray. So he did.

He had barely moved a muscle and Kathleen had hardly moved at all four hours later when Kim walked into the NICU. His whole body felt numb, but he wouldn't trade it for the world, and didn't want to let his daughter go.

Maybe Glenda had forgotten about them, but more than likely, all of Kathleen's vitals were going well, and she just let them stay the way they were. He'd been so careful to be still and not to upset anything, and maybe that was part of it too.

"You guys look so adorable together," Kim said, and he realized she had her phone in her hand and was taking a picture.

That made him grin at her. The idea that she wanted a picture of them together.

"Stay there, and we'll take a selfie too. I want to have a record of the first time her dad held her."

"I'm sorry. They offered, and I wasn't going to refuse."

"And I wouldn't have wanted you to. I'm just glad I was able to come and get some photos."

"I didn't think about pictures. I was just so happy to be able to hold her. She looks exactly like you."

"I hope not," Kim said, mock horror on her face. He laughed, mostly because it felt so good for Kim to have an expression on her face other than pain and worry.

They smiled for the pictures, and he thought about the day that Kathleen would look at them and how far away and long ago this day would feel. All the worry, all the care, everything that they were going through would be in the past.

Hopefully by then they would be a family.

He hadn't talked to Kim about getting married, but that was his end goal. He wanted to be a family. A real family. The three of them, and...maybe more. Together in Strawberry Sands.

But, he didn't want to upset the apple cart by pushing for that now. Kim was in no condition for more stress, and their focus had to stay on Kathleen.

But, he would say something. Eventually.

"I just unloaded the seventh load of hay in your barn." Matt Landry handed Davis the invoice he'd filled out before he left his farm.

"I appreciate it. Sorry I wasn't there to give you a hand."

"No problem," Matt said, and meant it. Sure, unloading it himself was a bit of a pain, and he was tired. "I totally get that you have a daughter in the NICU, and that's where your focus needs to be.

I'm just glad I can give you a hand and that I'm still young enough to unload it myself."

"If you look at yourself and consider yourself young, good for you," Davis said, smacking him on the back, as he took the invoice and picked up his checkbook.

Matt had told him he didn't need to pay right away, but Davis was the kind of man who liked to keep short accounts. That was the kind of man that Matt wanted to deal with. It was the kind of man he wanted to be. After all, wasn't a person supposed to be the kind of man they wanted to do business with?

They stood in the small office of the stable which was just down from the barn while Davis leaned over the small desk and wrote out a check.

"Wasn't there a little girl helping you the last time I was here? Somehow I got the idea she was your daughter, but they said around town that she wasn't."

"The joys of small town life. Everybody knows everything." Davis grinned, not the slightest bit upset that Matt had found out information about him in town. "She and her brother came and asked for a job, just right when I needed it. In fact, I think it might've been the day of or the day after Kathleen was born. I took them up on it right away and, I'll just be honest and say I've barely seen them. I pay her, and when I get home at night, I check to make sure the horses have feed and water, and they always do. The stalls always look great, cleaned out and with plenty of shavings, but nothing wasted. As far as I'm concerned, she does a great job, and I probably will pay her more when I get a chance to increase it. Although, I don't know how much she's doing and how much her brother's doing. She was pretty small."

"That's why I thought she was your daughter. She just looked a little young to be having a job. But, if she's doing that great, then she deserves it."

"Sometimes when people are small in stature, we have a tendency to base age on size."

"That's true. Although, I've not been around kids enough to be able to estimate their size and age with any accuracy anyway," Matt said, taking the check Davis handed him and thanking him. "You still want as much hay as I can bring you?"

"Until the barn is full. That'll save us from having to do it this winter. Although, I'll have to keep a road plowed from here to the barn, since we'll be hauling it down."

"Better hauling it from the barn than hauling it the whole way from my stable when there's two feet of snow on the beach."

"Do you get that much here?"

"Depends on the way the wind blows. If we get lake effect, we can get a ton, but if the wind is blowing a different direction, someone else gets it, which is just fine with me. If we get it for Christmas, and then it melts until the next year, I'm perfectly happy."

"Sounds to me like you're living in the wrong place if you don't want snow."

Matt laughed. "True. When you live on the shores of Lake Michigan, you need to expect that there is going to be cold weather and snow. I love it. I just don't really love working in it."

Davis nodded, and they walked toward the end of the stable together. A couple horses nickering as they walked by.

"Did you get your website uploaded?" Matt asked as they walked.

"I did. We even have some bookings. I'm not sure how I'm going to handle all of that, with taking Kim back and forth to the hospital, and spending a little time with Kathleen myself."

"If you need me to cover for you, I don't have a problem helping out."

"I don't want to take you from your family."

"It's just me. Well, my daughter will be coming and spending the summer with me like she always does. But beyond that, it's just me on the farm, so it's not a big deal."

"Your family runs a bed-and-breakfast, right?" Davis said, and Matt had to admit he was a little impressed. Since Davis hadn't been around for long, and hadn't been in town enough to hear all the gossip, it was pretty impressive that he remembered even that much.

"That's right. I help Mom some with that. We often get riders from our guests, and vice versa. All of the family helps with the farm in some way, but I really meant wife and kids aren't an issue, since I don't have any."

Davis nodded, and said, "If I get into a pickle, I'll give you a call. I appreciate everything you've done."

Matt didn't reply because just then a figure came to the end of the stable.

"Davis?" the woman asked, as though her eyes hadn't adjusted to the dim interior and she couldn't see where they were.

"Right here." The man beside him hurried forward, a new note in his voice, caring, concerned, and a tenderness that made Matt blink. He wasn't used to hearing men speak like that, but there could be no doubt that Davis adored Kim.

"Thanks for doing the laundry," she said, sounding a little out of breath like she just got more exercise that she was used to.

"Are you okay? I was coming right back in. I didn't want to make you walk the whole way out here."

"I'm fine. It hardly hurts at all anymore. And, I'd like to build my strength back up. I don't get the opportunity to do that when I'm sitting in the NICU with Kathleen."

"True, but I still don't want you to overdo it."

"I won't. Not from just walking out to the stable," Kim said, a smile in her voice.

Matt watched the two of them, and remembered that the folks in town had said that they weren't married. In his opinion they should be. They both were obviously quite fond of each other. More than fond it seemed like. He actually wouldn't mind having a woman look at him the way Kim looked at Davis. But, he'd already messed things up once in his life, and now his daughter had two homes she had to toggle back and forth between. That wasn't the way he wanted to raise his child, and he didn't want to make a mistake like that again.

Plus, how hard did a man have to look in order to find a woman who was interested in his welfare, and not just in his wallet? Who would look at him the way Kim was looking at Davis? So far in his thirty-some years of living, he hadn't found anyone like that, and he figured that the odds were probably pretty high that he wasn't going to.

"Give me a call if you need anything, I'll be bringing another load of hay in a couple of days. We're pretty booked up right now, but summer weekends are always busy." He walked up to the two of them, nodded his head at Kim and said, "Ma'am. Hope you're feeling better, and the baby too."

"Thanks," she glanced at him with a small smile, while her hand came up and landed on Davis's arm, where her fingers curled around his bicep.

Davis's hand came up and covered hers, while he gave Matt a nod.

"Thanks, man."

Matt nodded and walked away, lifting his hat and running a hand through his hair, before he got in his pickup.

He was grateful to have such great neighbors. He really hoped things worked out between them, because it was pretty obvious to him that the two of them belonged together.

Chapter 27

"I can't believe it's been six weeks!" Kristin said as she put a bite of salad in her mouth. Salad wasn't exactly the Strawberry Sands diner's specialty, but every once in a while, she tried to be healthy. Maybe it was something about her friend being in the hospital.

Kim nodded. "I'm able to hold her now. I can't believe how much she's grown. But honestly, just being able to touch her has been such a blessing. It was so hard in the beginning when all I could do was look at her and put a finger on her hand once in a while." She shivered.

Kristin had to hand it to Kim, she'd gone through the whole trial with so much beauty and grace, Kristin was almost jealous of the peace that seemed to radiate off of Kim.

"I can't wait to meet her. We've seen so many pictures, and I feel like I know her, but it'll be really sweet to actually be able to see her and to touch her," Heidi said, smiling at Kristin.

After Kim had had her baby, the folks in Strawberry Sands had gotten together, not just to help her, but to befriend her, since she was new in town.

Heidi owned the bookstore and souvenir shop, and along with Kristin, they had a weekly date with Kim on Wednesday nights. They hadn't really planned for it to be a weekly thing when they first asked her if they could take her out to eat on a particularly hard Wednesday when Davis had come into the diner and asked Griff and Charlotte to pray for Kim and Kathleen.

Heidi and Kristin had been in the diner, and they hadn't just prayed, they'd gone to the hospital and asked him if they could meet her in the chapel. That turned into an hours-long conversation, and they ended up taking Kim out to eat.

Funny sometimes how friendship started, but Kristin felt like theirs was a solid one that would last for years. She could see them growing old together.

"I can't wait to get home and have her life get back to normal. But is it crazy that I'm really enjoying this time in the hospital?"

"Yeah, that's not normal," Kristin said. She hated hospitals. She went to them when she had to, to visit and that type of thing, but the idea of herself being in a hospital was scary beyond words.

Maybe that was part of the reason she was currently eating a salad. It had less to do about staying healthy and more to do about a hospital phobia.

"You know, sometimes when you face your fears, you find out that they're not as bad as what you thought they were all along." Heidi shrugged. "Not that I know a whole lot about it, just... Maybe I know a little."

Kristin sat up a little straighter in her chair, wondering if Heidi was going to tell them a little bit about her backstory. How she came to Strawberry Sands and came to own the bookstore.

But Heidi smiled and shrugged her shoulders again. "Hopefully she'll get out in time for you to be able to enjoy summer. Summer on the beach is the best." She grinned, and Kim and Kristin both agreed with her.

Nothing like walking barefoot on the beach, the wind blowing their hair, the sun shining down, and the sound of the waves, rhythmic and soothing.

"I'd be a lot more concerned if it wasn't for Davis."

"You know he's head over heels for you," Kristin said, holding a forkful of onions in the air.

"I think he likes me okay, but I think head over heels is a little bit strong."

"Likes you okay?" Heidi said incredulously. "He's taking care of everything while you've been in the hospital, washing your clothes, starting a stable business, and you should see him anytime Kathleen takes a turn for the worse, he's in here looking haggard and worn. Like he's concerned about both of you. I don't know if I've ever seen anyone as devoted as him, and you guys aren't even married."

Kim looked down at her food, pushing it around her plate with her fork. She sighed and looked at her friends. "I know he's the real deal, but... You know how you've been through something once, and you put everything you had into it? How you just tried so hard, I mean, not tried to do something in your own power exactly, just knowing that marriage is hard, and you had to learn to forgive and let go and give up and learn to serve and to return unkindness with kindness and all that and you just try, putting everything you have into that one relationship and it doesn't work out."

She sighed again, a little softer, like she was tired, and then she said, "And you know how it just seems like so much work to do it again, and even though

I know Davis is a good man, so much different than my first husband, I just... I guess I just lost my blinders or something. Or maybe I'm just tired. Or maybe I'm just... I don't know. Maybe I'm scared. But I don't think that's it. I just don't want to put all of that work into another relationship that...fails."

She said the last word like she was looking for a different word but couldn't think of one.

Even if that wasn't the word she wanted, Kristen felt like she knew exactly what Kim was saying, but she hadn't given up on love the way it seemed like Kim had.

"Maybe you need to just give yourself a little bit of time," Heidi said. "I think you'll come around. Although... I hate to see you give yourself too much time and have Davis leave."

"Davis isn't going anywhere. Davis thinks Kim is the sun, moon, and stars. And he's the kind of guy who's going to love her till she dies. You can take as long as you want to. Davis will be there when you figure yourself out." Kristin was sure of what she was saying.

Kim looked at her thoughtfully. "I guess he will, won't he?" She smiled a little. "And that right there should be all it takes for me to know that he would be worth my effort. Worth going down that road again for. Because he wouldn't let me go. And he would do his very best to make sure our relationship works. He wouldn't leave all of that up to me while he just cruised on my shoulders."

"Exactly. You got that exactly right." Heidi nodded, as though she were just as sure as Kristin was that Davis was a good man.

They finished their meals, and then Heidi and Kim went out to Heidi's car while Kristin bid them good evening and started up the walk toward her house.

She'd inherited a big old house right on the main street of Strawberry Sands, and she hadn't quite figured out what she was going to do with it. She needed to figure something out. Turn it into a bed-and-breakfast maybe. Or... Something. She wasn't sure. But she needed to do something to start earning money.

Her phone rang as she stepped onto the wide front porch. It was beautiful with morning glory vines trailing up the trellis on one end while daylilies bloomed in profusion in the front. It was the kind of old house that would be in a 1950s sitcom with the woman in a white apron standing at the stove and her perfect children walking around while she kissed her husband who just came home from work.

It was the kind of house that Kristin never dreamed she would own.

She glanced at her phone, saw it was her grandmother, and slid to answer. "Hello?" she said.

"Krissy," her grandmother said in a tone that was so familiar it made Kristin's heart ache as her lips turned up in a smile.

"Gram. Are you still coming out to live with me?" Her parents had wanted to put her gram in a nursing home, but her gram was still spry, even though she was seventy-five years old. And she had absolutely no desire to be in a nursing home.

Her parents were insisting on it, but Kristin had intervened and said Gram could move in with her. After all, the house was big enough, and her gram could take care of herself. Her parents just didn't want her living alone. Not at her age.

"Well, that's what I was calling you about," Gram said, and just the tone of her voice made Kristin pause with her hand on the doorknob.

What in the world could Gram be up to now?

Her gram was known as being someone who had an irrepressible spirit. In her younger years, she traveled a lot, to countries that Kristin had to admit she had no desire to go to. Tajikistan, Greenland, and she even took a cruise to Antarctica.

"Okay. What's going on?"

"Well, I know that the house you inherited from your other grandmother has six bedrooms. How would you feel if I brought three of my friends with me?"

"Three?" Kristin said, a little surprised.

"Well, hear me out. Two of them need a place to stay, because they're in the same situation I am with their children. And one of them just wants to come with me. After all, I am known as somewhat of a good entertainer."

"I know you are, Gram." That was definitely the truth.

"They can pay. In fact, the money that we'd spend on nursing home care could be given to you, and you wouldn't have to do anything but chase after us all day."

Her gram said that like chasing after her and her friends would be somehow fun.

"Gram. I have a degree in graphic design. I can't..."

Maybe she could. Maybe she could have...what would it be called? An assisted care facility? Why couldn't she do that? She tilted her head, thinking. Maybe it wouldn't be such a bad idea. But before she made any decisions, she was going to need more information. Walking over to the swing, she sat down.

"Gram, do you think you could get your friends together, and we could have a meeting to talk about this? It'd be great if their kids could be there too so we could all be sure we are on the same page."

Sometimes it was hard to discern the will of the Lord, and then other times, He opened up the door so wide it was impossible not to get sucked through.

Kristin had the feeling that this was one of those times where she was going to get sucked through, whether she wanted to or not.

Chapter 28

"**I** can't believe we are finally home!" Kim said as they pulled into the drive,

"Eight weeks later," Davis said with a laugh. "You know, it feels like forever, and yet it feels like no time at all."

"They had so many instructions for us...do you think we're going to end up back there?"

"They said a high percentage of people who are discharged from NICU do come back, but that was because they didn't follow all the instructions. I think we're going to beat the odds."

"The biggest thing was to make sure she keeps eating and gaining weight."

"And that'll be your job. I'll try to make sure I take care of everything else so you can focus on that."

It had been such a disappointment when they'd finally started feeding Kathleen, and she wouldn't take anything but a bottle. She'd been bottle-fed for so long that she hadn't wanted anything else. Kim was still pumping, but she figured it was probably just a matter of time until she couldn't do everything, and she quit. After all, it would take twice as long to feed her if she had to pump and then turn around and give the bottle to Kathleen.

The nurses had told her not to worry about it, that she was doing everything she could for her baby, and if there were a couple of things that didn't work out, it certainly wasn't her fault. She knew that, but still, it had been a bitter disappointment.

Regardless, she knew Davis was right. She would just focus on doing her very best, following the instructions to the letter, and keep them safe and healthy.

"Look at that," Kim exclaimed, pointing down toward the beach where a group of five people rode horseback right along the edge where the waves met the shore. It was beautiful against the blue of the lake and sky, and there were smiles on all of their faces as they rode toward them.

"Isn't it beautiful?" Davis said, looking up and smiling. "This is a really satisfying business. You wouldn't believe the smiles on people's faces. And, it's a lot of fun to watch. You can see it really well from the back porch of the cottage."

He paused, then he said, "It's probably an even better view from up in the loft above the stable, although the window isn't as big."

"About that," Kim started. She...did not know how to approach the subject. Davis had been so helpful and solicitous toward her the entire time Kathleen had been in the hospital. But he hadn't said anything more about possibly getting married, or even about having a relationship. She didn't know what to term what they had right now. Friends for sure, but she didn't know whether he considered her more. Maybe he changed his mind. He'd seen her at her very worst, while he had appeared strong and capable the entire time. Tired at times, perhaps, but not like she had been - in pain, anxious, and overwhelmed.

"Let's get inside. I have some things I want to talk to you about." Davis's words were low, and to her ear they gave no hint as to what he was actually thinking.

Could he want to discuss how they would split up their time with Kathleen?

Surely not. He hadn't breathed the word about that the entire time she'd been in the hospital, but of course, he'd been going out of his way to keep her calm and to have her not worry about anything.

She appreciated everything he'd done so much, but maybe he figured now that they were home it was time to have a serious discussion about their roles.

She took a breath. She wasn't going to borrow trouble. Of course she wanted to be more, wanted to do more, wanted to have more with him. How could she not after the way he'd been for the last eight weeks?

But, she'd been on the receiving end of most everything, and she hadn't been able to give back much.

Maybe he was going to talk to her about that. That he was tired of having a one-sided relationship, and was going to hand everything over to her and leave.

Again, she knew she was borrowing trouble. Why did she always go to the worst case scenario? Had he ever acted like he didn't like her? On the contrary, he'd been so tenderly loving and caring, had hinted about more, although he'd never come out and said it.

It could go that way too.

She pushed her car door open, and grabbed the baby bag and another bag that had all of their hospital paraphernalia in it while Davis unhooked Kathleen who had slept the whole way home and pulled her car seat out.

"It wasn't quite the homecoming that you had planned, I'm sure, but we're home. And I think that's what matters." He grinned at her, and despite the fear that churned in her chest, she smiled back.

"Kim?" he asked, as though he could read on her face that all was not well.

"I guess when people say they want to talk to me, I just always assume that I'm in trouble. Or that it's something bad."

He laughed a little. "And here I thought I was the one who was nervous and scared. And you were just as cool as a cucumber over there."

"I might be a cucumber, but I'm not feeling very cool."

He laughed again. "I just want more. I don't want to push you, and I don't want to make you make decisions that you're not ready for, but these last eight weeks with you and Kathleen have made it easy for me to know that I want a family, and I want it with you. Not just because Kathleen is the most adorable baby in the entire world," he said, as she fell into step beside him and they walked up the walk, all of her fear melting away.

"I told myself that I didn't need to worry about you leaving us, but that was what I was afraid of."

"I guess I can blame that on Todd. But, you don't have to worry about me leaving. Even if you don't want me, I don't want to leave. I'm staying as long as you let me."

"Thank you. I might need that reassurance a few more times before I actually believe it. Actually, a lot more times maybe."

"I'm staying. I'm staying. And I want to stay with you." He puffed out a laugh, as they stopped in front of the locked front door. He pulled the key out of his pocket, holding the car seat. "I don't want to keep Kathleen outside, but, I hadn't intended to say this now, but...will you marry me?"

She couldn't help the gasp that she choked on and then coughed and sputtered as her eyes watered. "Okay. Sure."

"I didn't mean to choke you. I hope that was a good choking? If there is such a thing?"

"The very best kind of choking," she said, nodding, before she coughed a little more.

"That was the very worst proposal in the history of the world. I know it. I am not good at this, but I guess I just wanted it so bad that I couldn't stand here and pretend that I didn't. Especially when you were nervous about what I was going to say. Please don't be nervous. I... I admire you, and want to be a part of your life. Want to be a part of Kathleen's as well. Want to have a family, and I want that to be with you."

"Oh...well. I'm feeling a little over-whelmed. But I definitely want all that with you."

He leaned over the baby carrier, and pressed his lips to hers. She closed her eyes, savoring the gentle feeling, and the way she always felt cared for and cherished when Davis was near.

"You make me feel like you really love me."

"I do. I love you. More than anything."

"I love you too. How could I not? You've been better to me than anyone in the world ever has been, and, when I'm with you, I feel like we could be a family."

"That's what I want."

He leaned back a little, and they smiled into each other's eyes.

A small "woof," made both of them turn their heads.

"That's a dog," Kim said, knowing that they were both looking at a big white shaggy…

"A Great Pyrenees?" Davis said, scrunching his face up a little as though trying to figure out if that might be what it was.

"Yes. I believe so."

"I heard they're very friendly, but honestly I haven't seen this one around at all. Once we're in and settled, maybe I'll give Matt a call, or Griff at the diner, and see if they know anyone who's missing one."

"All right. That sounds good. He looks like he needs a home."

"Guess we need a dog," he said, looking at Kim with his brows raised.

"I guess we do. We have a baby, and I suppose it would take a dog to make our family complete."

"A dog, ten horses, a baby and a wife. You said you'd marry me? I didn't dream that?"

"I will. Whenever you want."

"We should plan a wedding," he said as he put the key in the lock and opened the door.

"Or we could just do it."

"You wouldn't want something fancy?"

"No. Nothing fancy. Just you."

That made him smile, as he pushed the door open and she stepped into her home, her husband to be, and her baby coming in behind her.

The sooner they were a real family, the better. It felt perfect.

"That was a good homecoming," she said, turning around as Davis set the still sleeping Kathleen on the floor, and gathered Kim up in his arms.

"I think we can make it better," he murmured as his head descended toward hers.

"I think you might be right," she whispered before his lips covered hers and his arms pulled her tight, as her hands went around his neck, tugging his head closer and pressing her body against his. Memories of the night they spent together spun in her head reminding her that everything was just as good, maybe even better, than what she remembered.

But that was just a small part of the reason that she loved Davis. Just because he was a good kisser, wasn't enough. Todd could probably be considered a good kisser. Davis was everything Todd wasn't, and so much more.

But then she stopped thinking, and just focused on kissing him back.

Epilogue

"**I** think we should have a party."

Davis sat on the back deck, the full moon shining off a smooth-as-silk Lake Michigan, the night breeze gently drifting off the water and the woman he loved snuggled in his arms. He couldn't think of how he could be happier.

"A party?" he repeated, although he knew he'd heard her just fine. He wasn't really thinking about a party. He was thinking more about a wedding. He'd just asked her to marry him the day before, but with getting Kathleen settled and making sure everything was going to go well with her, and of course Bev and Bill had stopped in to visit - which Davis was happy about. It made Kim happy to see her parents, happy to know that they loved and cared for her. But with all that, they'd not talked much about a date. It couldn't be soon enough for him.

"To celebrate our wedding. Well, maybe to celebrate bringing Kathleen home, too. It's been a long journey."

"It sure has." He couldn't agree more. "So…do you think we should get married before we plan a party to celebrate our marriage?"

She chuckled softly, the sound sweet and beautiful on the night air. "We need to fix that."

"Us not being married?"

"Yes. Don't you think so?"

"I do." Boy, did he ever.

"Today, Kathleen's first day home from the hospital went pretty well. What do you say we take her for her first car ride and go to the courthouse tomorrow?"

"I say let's do it."

She turned her head slightly and kissed the side of his neck. "You are a very reasonable man."

"I'm a man who's in love with a very amazing woman. A man who can't believe his good fortune, but wants to enjoy whatever God throws his way."

She sighed. "Did you see the look on Bill's face when I called him 'Dad' today?"

"It was even more surprised than Bev's look when you called her 'Mom.'"

"After the way they helped us, after all they've done, after they've supported me, called and texted and just sat with me when I needed someone to lean on, how could I not embrace them? I just wasn't sure how they'd feel about it, and…I was afraid to ask. I honestly hadn't even meant to say it, but it just felt right. Is that crazy?"

"No. I don't think so at all. Bill and Bev have stepped up and been the best parents you could ever ask for. It's obvious they love you and they love Kathleen, too."

"I think they're pretty fond of you as well."

"Ha. You think so?" He loved Bev, but Bill still made him a little nervous, like he was watching Davis to make sure he did right by his daughter. Davis had every intention of doing right by Kim - like he hadn't before - which is why he straightened. "I'd better head back over to the stable."

"There is something really wrong with that sentence."

"Tomorrow night I can say we should head to bed."

"I think there is a three day waiting period."

"Three days feels like forever."

"It does." She sighed as he stood, then slowly stood with him. "Thank you for being here. I would have been scared to be by myself, but it was so much easier to know I could count on you if I needed to."

"If she wakes up and you want me to come over, just call me, okay? I'll keep my phone by my bed." So far the monitor on the picnic table in front of them had been quiet.

"I will. She slept until three am last night. But she'd been sleeping through the night in the hospital, so maybe she'll start doing that again."

"I hope so." He didn't want Kim to wear herself out. Bev and Bill and he had all worked to make sure she got enough rest, although she desperately wanted to be by Kathleen's side herself all the time. And the town of Strawberry Sands had rallied around them, providing food and mowing their grass and making sure they knew they were loved and cared for and that they were praying for them.

"We should name that dog," Kim said as she slipped an arm around him and lay her head on his chest, looking toward the driveway where the Great Pyerenes lay beside their car. In the morning he'd be gone. And so would the dog food they'd set out for him.

"Someone should. I'm not sure he's ours. He seems to belong to the town."

"I like that. He's like a lifeguard, only on land. I do feel safer when he's around."

"And he seems to know we needed a little extra watching lately."

"He does." She leaned back and looked up at him. "Thank you for being such an amazing father. Kathleen is well and truly blessed."

"Hopefully I'll be an even better husband." He hoped so. Kim deserved the very, very best. He wanted to give it to her.

"You will. I know without a doubt that you will." She reached up and touched her lips with his. It was a while before he remembered that he needed to go to his own place for the night. But, eventually he did remember, making sure Kim was safely inside before he did. Three more days. He couldn't wait.

Thanks so much for reading! If you'd like to continue reading about the folks in Strawberry Sands, you can get the next book .

If you'd like to stay up on all things Jessie, sign up for my newsletter or join my Patreon community .

Enjoy this preview of There I Find Peace, just for you!

Chapter 1

Jubilee's car sputtered.

You have got to be kidding me.

She didn't open her mouth because her two daughters, Scarlett and Penelope, sat in the backseat. They'd been driving for twelve hours, and they were both exhausted.

Her car sputtered again and her fingers tightened on the steering wheel.

Please, Lord. Just ten more miles.

She glanced at the gas gauge, which showed it to have about a sixteenth of a tank, just slightly above the bottom Empty line.

That was one sixteenth, wasn't it?

Maybe that was wishful thinking.

"Mom is the car going to break down?" Scarlett said from her position behind Jubilee's seat.

"I hope not," Jubilee gave her the honest answer.

"I hope it does. I'm sick of sitting in here." Penelope, eight, never hesitated to speak her mind.

She wanted to tell Penelope to keep her hopes to herself, because if their car broke down, it was going to be a very long time before Jubilee's day was over, and considering that twelve hours of driving would wear out anyone, she was ready for the day to be over. Ready for the week to be over. Ready for her life... She didn't want to think that, so she pulled those words back into her brain.

Truly, she didn't think things could get any worse. She wondered how long she was going to be living at the bottom, where things couldn't get any worse.

The car sputtered one more time, then the engine died.

All right, so when the gas gauge was just a little bit above the line, it didn't mean that there was one sixteenth of a gallon tank left. It meant that the little arrow couldn't go any lower.

At least the highway was wide and flat, unlike some of the hills that they'd been driving in earlier that day as they left Pennsylvania.

Those roads had a tendency to be winding and narrow, with high bridges that took her breath away, and made her want to close her eyes.

Michigan was much different. Especially here along the lake. Strawberry Sands was just ten miles or so away, and it was right on the shore of Lake Michigan.

Lord, I was hoping we would make it. I thought you were going to help us get there. Wasn't that the deal? I would put everything I had into it, if you would just get us to Strawberry Sands.

She hadn't been sure at the time if God was really making that deal with her, or if she just really wanted the change of pace herself.

Strawberry Sands was one of the few happy memories she had from her childhood, a place of peace and comfort. A place where neighbors cared about each other, and where it was safe to walk the streets. A place she'd like to raise her girls. Now that she finally left her cheating husband.

There is no point in thinking about that now. Currently, she had a problem sitting in front of her that she was going to have to solve before she got to go to bed tonight. If she even got to go to bed. After all, she wouldn't have run out of gas if she would have had the money to fill up her tank back in Blueberry Beach, when they passed the last gas station.

She'd been hoping to get to Strawberry Sands, hoping to get a job. Hoping to... She didn't know. She really didn't have plans for tonight, which probably showed what a terrible parent she actually was. But, in a place like Strawberry Sands, they could sleep in their car, they could sleep along the beach, either place would be just as safe as sleeping in a two-story house with a white picket fence in the middle of small-town USA.

Still, normal adults didn't plan to house their children in their car for any length of time, even just one night.

Maybe she would have been better off staying with her husband.

Or at the very least, staying with her mother-in-law. Which was where she moved when she found out that her husband had been cheating.

Not a smart move, since two nights ago, her mother-in-law had invited her husband and his new girlfriend over for dinner. She had expected Jubilee to have the girls at the table, and to be welcoming to their "guest."

Jubilee knew that as a Christian she needed to be kind, but as a human, her heart just hurt too hard for her to do much more than sit at the table and try not to cry.

She got up to get the dessert, and instead of getting it and taking it back into the table, she slipped up the back stairs, going to her room, and doing that very thing.

Hopefully God would understand. Actually, she knew He did. Jesus went through a trail at his crucifixion that had to have been just as painful. The Bible didn't record him crying, but that doesn't mean he didn't.

After living through what she had, Jubilee suspected he had.

She fingered her cell phone as she sat along the road.

"Mom? What are you going to do?" Scarlett asked, and her voice didn't sound sweet and nice. It sounded rather demanding, like she expected her mother to fix this problem and now.

"You need to call a tow truck. He needs to have someplace to haul all of us to. Make sure of that when you call them." Penelope had to put her two cents in too. She acted older than an eight-year-old, probably because she was so smart. Jubilee wasn't sure where she got her intelligence, since it certainly wasn't from her. She was about the dumbest person in the world, and anyone who doubted it could just look at the decisions she made over the course of her life, if they needed to be convinced.

This latest decision, the one that made her just jump in her car and take off, was case in point. Although, where she ended up started out with her decision to not open a new bank account only in her name.

She had had almost a thousand dollars, which wasn't a whole lot, but it was everything that she'd saved since she left her husband. She'd had to pay the lawyers fees since her husband filed for divorce. And that had set her back or she would have had more. Still, it had been a shock at noon when her card had been declined when she tried to buy lunch at a fast food place along the interstate.

After doing some research, she realized that her husband had taken everything but ten bucks from the account.

She assumed it was him, since no one else had access to it. She had thought it was fraud, and considered reporting it, but she would have felt like an idiot if the bank had said that it was her husband who took it. Still, she called, just to confirm. The lady at the bank had been super helpful. After all, she'd known Jubilee for years, since that's where they'd banked since they got married.

The lady had cheerfully informed Jubilee that her husband had, indeed, taken the money.

It was not coming back. And Jubilee knew there was nothing she could do about it. She wasn't the kind of person to beat a dead horse.

If she were, she might take this opportunity to cry. But of course, crying didn't solve anyone's problems, and she really didn't have time for that right now anyway. Actually, she did have time.

"I'm hungry," Scarlett whined from the back seat.

Okay. Maybe she didn't have a lot of time.

She sighed and tried to think of whether or not there was still a small package of peanuts in her purse. She couldn't even remember where she got, but she did remember digging around them more than once, thinking that she should just take them out, and then reminding herself that someday she might want them.

She reached over the consol, picked up her purse which sat on the passenger side.

Her wallet was in there of course, but it was empty.

After digging for a bit, she found a package of peanuts.

"This is all I have. It should tide you over until we figure things out."

She should call a tow, but she didn't have the money to pay. She didn't even have a credit card because when she left her husband, she'd cut them all up, knowing she couldn't afford to rack up a bunch of debt.

Buying things she didn't need wasn't exactly something she did a lot of, but she didn't want to be tempted. Tempted to buy things for her children to try to diminish the pain of not having a father living with them anymore.

Back when she was a young mother, back when she had stars in her eyes and dreams of being the best mom anyone had ever had, she'd determined in her heart that she would be a happy mom. Someone who made everything fun. Someone whom her children remembered us smiling every day and laughing freely.

Of course there were times when a person had to be serious, but she didn't want her children to remember her as someone who never laughed, or smiled, or had fun.

She wanted them to remember their childhood as joyful and happy.

She almost laughed. How could a child remember their childhood as joyful and happy when their parents split right in the middle of it, breaking up their home, and tearing up everything that they thought was dependable and safe?

Still, her goal of being happy and joyful was still attainable, just harder.

For the most part she felt like she'd done pretty well, but... It was always an effort. Especially at times like these when she really didn't know what to do, and she was scared and sad and alone.

"All right girls, we're going to get to walk a little bit. The lake breeze always feels fresh and clean and the first person who sees Lake Michigan gets a star."

"Mom. We're too old for the star thing," Scarlett said and if a voice could roll its eyes, hers was rolling all over the place.

"All right. That's fine. If you don't want to start, I can give one to myself. Because I'm pretty sure I'm going to see the lake first," she said easily, opening up her door and stepping out. Her purse was the only thing of any value that she would want to take with her, but they probably should take a change of clothes as well.

Walking back to the trunk, she popped the hood and pulled her suitcase around so she could open it.

"Could someone just pick us up and give us a ride?" Scarlett said.

"Why aren't you calling a tow truck, mom?" Penelope asked, as her girls came around the back of the truck car.

She hadn't wanted them to worry about money. She hadn't wanted them to worry about anything. She wanted their childhoods to be safe and happy and secure. But what she wanted, and what actually happened were obviously not going to be the same thing.

"I don't want to call a tow truck when I can't pay them for what they're going to do," she said matter-of-factly so that it didn't worry the girls. She had learned that it seemed like if she acted worried, then they became worried as well.

"So what are we gonna do?" Scarlett asked, probably understanding the implications of the fact that they couldn't afford to pay for a tow better than her younger sister. Even if her younger sister was the one who usually had something to say about it.

"And pray as we walk. We're going to be happy that we have legs. Happy that it's a beautiful summer day, and not the middle of winter. It's cold up here in the winter. With lots of snow."

"I love snow!" Penelope said. "How soon is it going to snow?"

"Well, I'm not sure. I've never been here when it snows. But it's June, so probably not until fall."

She looked back down at the suitcase. "I'm going to pull an outfit for each of us that we can wear tomorrow, plus our night things." The girls talked a bit as they chose an outfit to take, and Jubilee put them in a plastic bag grocery store bag.

They hadn't passed a single car for the last ten minutes they'd been driving, and no one had passed them since they had pulled over to the side of the road, so when she heard a motor floating over the quiet of the lake air, she picked her head up.

Should she try to stop them?

It turned out like so many things in her life she worried about - it resolved on its own.

When she straightened and turned around, the pickup coming toward her already had its turn signal on and was slowing down.

She supposed she probably should have been scared, but it made her smile. This was what Strawberry Sands was to her. People stopping to help other people, even if they were complete strangers. The townsfolk helped each other even more.

It was the kind of community she wanted to be a part of.

Still, she was expecting a kindly older gentleman, or maybe even a teenager, but the man who pulled up behind her and stepped out of her pickup, was in his late twenties or early thirties, and handsome, as he shoved the cowboy hat down over his head and slammed his door closed. The stubble on his jaw was enough to make Jubilee's heart beat faster before she reminded her heart that handsome jaws and charming men made terrible husbands.

She would be the expert in that.

Her girls pushed closer to her side as the man walked toward them. His hand came out, and he lifted the brim of his hat just a little.

"I'm Matt. Looks like you might be needing some help."

Matt. She highly doubted it was the same Matt that she'd crushed on years ago, when she had spent the summer in Strawberry Sands. That was not why she was coming back. But, she couldn't deny there was a part of her that long for those sweet summer days when she sat on the beach and admired him as he rode his horse up and down the shore-line.

There were surfers in the water, boaters as well, but it was Matt and his horse that had always caught her eye.

"I'm Jubilee, and yeah. Unfortunately, I seem to have made bad decision after bad decision and am once more against the wall."

His face was serious, but one side of his mouth turned up, and her heart started beating hard again. It didn't seem to listen to anything she said. That didn't mean she had to do whatever it wanted to. In fact, in her experience, she was better off if she did the exact opposite.

Pick up your copy of There I Find Peace by Jessie Gussman today!

Escape to more faith-filled romance series by Jessie Gussman!

The Complete Sweet Water, North Dakota Reading Order:

Series One: Sweet Water Ranch Western Cowboy Romance (11 book series)

Series Two: Coming Home to North Dakota (12 book series)

Series Three: Flyboys of Sweet Briar Ranch in North Dakota (13 book series)

Series Four: Sweet View Ranch Western Cowboy Romance

Spinoffs and More! Additional Series You'll Love:

Jessie's First Series: Sweet Haven Farm (4 book series)

Small-Town Romance: The Baxter Boys (5 book series)

Bad-Boy Sweet Romance: Richmond Rebels Sweet Romance (3 book series)

<u>Sweet Water Spinoff: Cowboy Crossing (9 book series)</u>

<u>Holiday Romance: Cowboy Mountain Christmas (6 book series)</u>

<u>Small Town Romantic Comedy: Good Grief, Idaho (5 book series)</u>

<u>True Stories from Jessie's Farm: Stories from Jessie Gussman's Newsletter (3 book series)</u>

<u>Reader-Favorite! Sweet Beach Romance: Blueberry Beach (8 book series)</u>

<u>Cowboy Mountain Christmas Spinoff: A Heartland Cowboy Christmas (9 book series)</u>

<u>Blueberry Beach Spinoff: Strawberry Sands (8 book series)</u>

newsletter – I laughed so hard I sprayed it out all over the table!"

Claim your free
book from Jessie!

9 781953 066527